Presenting

Dom Wars
Round One

By
Lucian Bane

Acknowledgements

To the real life Tara… my beautiful wife… who made the impossible-- possible.
I love you.

Chapter One

The newspaper went into the recycling bin with a crisp snap. I usually ignored the book reviews, but one of the titles intrigued me, *The True Dom.* The reviewer had given it five stars and written a glowing commentary about the author's brilliance. I thought, maybe, just maybe someone gave a different portrayal of those in the Dominate/submit lifestyle. Wishful thinking. It was just another compilation of fuck-font, confusing a Dick with a Dom.

The lifestyle had become ridiculously overrun with fake Doms exploiting the pool of victims ignorantly, and sometimes openly, begging to be brutalized. And with the fifty shades of kink epidemic, the shit had exploded and people flocked to it with barely a clue what they were getting into. The result was a feeding frenzy of epic proportion with untold carnage.

The wastebasket was nearly empty, but I bundled the items to drop off to the recycling center anyway. The urge to clean *something,* or put one thing *right* in the

3

world, was more than I could stand. A bold heading on the back of the newspaper I'd thrown away caught my eye. **"Dom Wars"**. I snatched the newspaper out and read.

Do you naturally Dominate others? Do you get your way through control and discipline? Do others look to you for leadership?

If so, prove it and win $1,000,000!

Audition to compete on a reality TV show and prove to the world that you have what it takes to Dominate!

The Ultimate Dom wins and will become the new face and spokesperson for the alternative lifestyle division of Gladiator, Inc., producer of bestselling adult novelties and toys.

I stood riveted in pure *what the fuck, no way in hell,* shock. The piece went on to list terms and conditions and disclaimers, which I barely skimmed. Holy shit. They had to be kidding.

A million? The idea of that much money began to dance in my head. Who couldn't use that? I stared at the ad, halfway chewing on my lower lip. The need to conquer infused my bones and suddenly pulsated like a powerhouse of influence in my cock. Challenge of any and every kind had always drawn me, fueled by some vague need to prove myself. The true test became choosing the wisest challenge.

This was definitely a worthy *and* wise challenge. Becoming the Ultimate Dom? The face of Gladiator, Inc.? Eh. Everything had its con.

I jotted down the *call for more details* number, ready to learn what exactly this DOM WARS would require of me. Even though I'd been out of the lifestyle for several years, it shouldn't be a problem. Like riding a bike, for the most part. And my Dom wasn't a role I played, it was my nature. If it was an authentic gig, I should be fine. But until I knew that, the thoughts creating a lightning storm in my head would have to simmer.

****

All the possibilities Dom Wars might entail absorbed my mind as I jogged around the lake at the park a few blocks from my apartment. Images of sweaty bodies in soft light, the sound of leather smacking flesh, moans of pain mingled with pleasure, and a myriad of other scenes I'd participated in through the years, flashed through my head.

The memory of a woman's ass as I soothed away the sting of a spanking, drove heat straight to my cock. The thrill of a submissive's ultimate trust in me as she gave herself over entirely to the pleasure I could bring her, made my heart pound. It also brought the empty feeling I slept with every night, no matter how much sex there was. It was as if I ate, but the food left by some hole in my stomach, never providing satisfaction or nourishment. It created a hungry monster inside me.

My hot shower sluiced away the sweat, but not the memories. The scenes playing out in my mind made my cock throb even though I knew indulging never answered that fucking need I couldn't name. And there was no more ignoring it. It'd dominated me. Bent me to its mysterious will, drove me out of the Dom lifestyle and into a soul search for who and what the fuck I really was. There was a war of wills inside me. Against my Dom and this… other consuming force. There needed to be a truce between the two or a fucking beat down. I wanted my body and mind back.

Still semi-erect and nude, I headed to the bedroom and dropped to the bed, head hanging. Water droplets fell to my bare legs, those images returning to torment me. And not just images. I could practically feel the warm puffy flesh of a just-spanked ass, begging my touch to sooth the sting away. *Just jack the fuck off and get it done.*

I closed my eyes, hating that it was difficult for me. But it was. I couldn't seem to convince my stupid Dom brain that it wasn't a fight I'd lost, or me licking my wounds.

I sat there, torn with the need to crush my own dominance, my own stupid reasoning. I laid back in an act of self-defiance and drew my knees up. Needing to get away from the reality, I closed my eyes. Bodies flashed in my mind and I grabbed my cock in one hand and cupped my balls with the other.

I searched my memory for the right fantasy, stroking myself. Women bound in various positions. I clenched my eyes tighter, focusing on their moans, the looks on their faces in ecstasy. My cock throbbed with life and I let my knees fall open as I listened to the sounds of her moans, delicate at first. I loved those.

Another sound encroached on my fantasy, deeper, sultrier. The woman who'd nearly crushed my balls.

Like a deflating tire, the desire left me. I sat up with a growl and scrubbed both hands over my head. Too many fucking memories. Too many women.

The phone rang and I walked nude to the other side of the couch in the living room and picked up the handset. "Yeah?"

A moment of silence and then, "Hello son. Tell me, why do you insist on answering the phone with such a disrespectful tone?"

I closed my eyes. Why didn't I fucking look at the caller ID? I hurried to my room for a robe, feeling like he could see and was sneering at my body. Not bulky enough. Like a little swimmer, he'd say. "Well hi, Dad. Good to hear from you, too." I kept my voice smooth as silk, refusing to give him the flat monotone he'd insisted I use all my life whenever I spoke with him. "Did you really call just to annoy yourself with my lack of phone etiquette?"

The way his breathing changed sent a little thrill of triumph through me. The chase was on, reminding me of my teen years. When my dominance set in, I subconsciously provoked him, then ran like hell. Mostly to take his brutal focus off my siblings.

He grunted. "Actually, I'm calling about your mother. Her birthday, rather. Her sixtieth is coming up next month and your sisters are organizing a party for her." He paused as if to let that sink in. "You will attend, of course, and without your usual arrogance and disrespect. I will not tolerate any sort of disruption or anything that might distress your mother. Hannah will contact you this afternoon with the specifics. Shall I arrange a female companion? Or are you capable of finding a suitable date yourself?"

The last time I'd gone home, my then-sub accompanied me. The old man had been deeply offended at her blatant disregard for him while her deference to me was obvious. "I'm sure I can manage that one myself." I waited to see what else he would say.

For a moment he remained silent. "And Lucian? Don't disappoint her any further. I presume you are still pretending to be a journalist?"

I hardened my jaw to prevent the sarcastic reply from flying out of my mouth. What would he say if I told him her disappointment stemmed from his open dislike for their child? Freelance journalism didn't count with him, no matter the money it made. He probably thought I whored for rent and really, that was more than fine by me, funny even. I remembered the audition for the adult toy company and suddenly, winning that reality show and having my face plastered all over the country by some dildo dot com was all so very sweet.

When I didn't rise to the bait, he continued as if we were chatting about the weather. "By the way, who is Jude Flerk? He's called my private line several times, trying to reach you. He said it was a matter of life and death for Little Sister and Momma, whoever that is. Something about new owners of Hank Delacour's business. You need to tell him to not call this number again."

A cold frisson of dread shot down my spine. Dear God. Several of my subs had come to me with habits, and like any good, ignorant Dom, I provided what they needed. I finally realized, I was only enabling them into the graves, but by that time, I'd ran through my small inheritance from Aunt Alexis. A lot of the subs had become addicts and like any addict, they did what they had to for a fix. Even charge it to my tab without me knowing. Either I paid or the subs did and I couldn't let that happen. I considered it miraculous that Hank, the pusher, was a halfway decent man and let me make notes. Fuck, this was bad news.

I assured my father I'd handle it and we said our stiff cordial goodbyes and hung up. Thank God.

I went to the bedroom and dressed, contemplating the possibilities and opportunities of the reality show. Fuck. Getting paid to get under the old man's skin was no longer on my mind. Fucking drug debts for drugs I never used would be my downfall. I needed to make a real effort of winning the fucking competition.

Chapter Two

"Ma'am. Ma'am! Line's moving."

I snapped to attention and closed the gap, then assessed the number of people standing around for nearly two hours. So much for thinking I could get some kind of early-bird advantage at the audition. I put my nose back in my Kindle, devouring every letter of the BDSM lifestyle manual. I was on my third read and that's all it would take to be able to ace any test they threw my way.

I discreetly snuck my eyeballs to the woman and man behind me wearing poorly stitched black shiny leather. It was just the right amount of strange that you wanted to stare and see what exactly was wrong with it. Most of the people there wore things that looked like costumes for a Halloween party. Corsets and high heels, leather pants, studded collars and heavy chains. Clothes for another species, it seemed.

Laughter came from somebody down the line behind me. The strong deep sound compelled me to lean over and try to locate the source.

"The line's moving, sugar." The gravelly voice of the man at my back startled me and I dropped my damn Kindle.

I lurched for it, praying it hadn't cracked, and my backpack toppled off my shoulder and onto the ground, sending my little tin of lucky pennies exploding out of the thing. Geeze. "Go around, go around." I shooed the people waiting behind me. "Just… keep driving."

I snuck glances around me, not letting my gaze get much higher than knees as I collected the cute little third grader tin can and change scattered to kingdom come. I felt like a beggar, picking up pennies someone flung at me. Gramma insisted I take it to my awesome new job interview in the next town over that paid so much money she'd be out of the nursing home in a month if I got it. It was cruel to give her that kind of hope but damn it, I couldn't help it, she needed it so badly. We both did.

Jesus there were a *lot* of knees and legs. *Don't look at the competition.* I was ready to leave the rest of the change on the ground, but with my luck, somebody would say hey, you missed some and then I'd have to talk to them. Wasn't happening.

I glanced at the front of the line and calculated the distance *into* the audition. Fifteen minutes maybe. Fear cut at my stomach.

"Need some help?" A man stooped next to me, directing his intense blue gaze at me.

"Uh. Thank you." I continued picking up the change, realizing I'd misspoken. No thank you was the intended response. And now he was helping me pick up my lunch money.

It was so awkward, there were no words. I hurried through the humiliation as fast as I could and before I knew it, he held his hand out to give me the money. I was suddenly terrified to touch him. "Keep it. For your help."

His hand remained, no doubt in confusion, because who gave you their spilled pennies after you helped pick them up? Girls from Missouri with social paranoia with men. Handsome men with blue eyes. Black hair. What was he doing there, anyway? He didn't match the crowd. I hurried back in line, leaving him to deal with the handful of unwanted change.

"No cutting."

I looked at the woman who'd spoken. "I was in line."

"I didn't see you." The deep voice came from a few feet back.

I searched for the couple I'd been near and suddenly finding the two odd people in the sea of oddness was the last thing I wanted to do in that second. I made my way to the end of the long line. It'd give me more time to study. Good.

I froze when the hunk who'd helped me pick up spare change approached. *Eyes on Kindle. Studying.*

"You mind if I tag along? I'm not in a big hurry."

Something in his tone drew my gaze. "You're not here for the audition?"

"Oh, yeah, I am…" He shrugged a little and lowered his head with a cute smile before angling his eyes at me, his look sending my heart to my stomach. "Came to win a million dollars. You?"

The mention of money woke me from my dork daze. "Yes, me too."

He chuckled and turned an exact gaze on me. "You realize we can't both win, right?"

I nodded slowly then more firmly.

"You have a plan?"

Realization bloomed all bubbly inside. This was the informant I so desperately needed for all those questions I didn't dare ask out loud. "I plan to win?"

He grinned all cute, his brows raising over mirthful blue eyes. "How do you plan to do that?"

"How do you?"

He threw his head back and gave that laugh I'd heard earlier. Now I wondered who had made him do that before and a twinge of something like jealously ran through me. He put his arm around my shoulder and whispered at my ear, "Sweetheart... what are you doing here?"

A million signals went off in my mind and body like fireworks, all shooting in crazy directions. Threat. Friend. Threat. Friend. Confusion blared all over the place. The low husky tone was the threat and it sent electricity arcing through all my nerve endings, practically begging for his touch. But the kindness, the concern, maybe some compassion, was the friend. The friend I desperately needed.

I regained my backbone and removed his arm from around me. "I came to win. I told you."

He put his hands in his black slacks, biting the corner of his full lower lip.

I eyed his outfit. "You're dressed differently than everyone else."

"So are you."

I snorted at the understatement. "I don't dress to impress."

"Really. What do you dress for?"

I looked at him, puzzled with his genuine tone. "For me." I looked him over deliberately, allowing my gaze to linger at certain points. "Who do you dress for?"

"For me as well." He was smiling like he had a secret about me that I didn't know.

I rested my case with a little salute.

"Subs usually dress for their Doms."

Ah. He was going to dig. "That's nice." I'd let him dig a bit and see how much I could learn before asking questions.

17

"So you're saying you came without your Dom." The corners of his luscious mouth tipped upward, just the barest hint of a smile.

"No," I corrected in a sweet voice. "I'm saying I'm my own Dom."

There he went with that amazing laugh again, the one that reached out and stroked you. Only this time it was accompanied with the burn of shame you get when somebody laughs in your face at how stupid you are.

"What?" I didn't hide my annoyance and he laughed more like I was just a piece of work.

"What?" He looked at me, all Mr. Perplexed to the extreme. "Your own *Dom*?"

I turned away from his dumbfounded raised brows. He thought I was stupid. I could see it, even hear it in his theatrical tone. "You find that funny, I see. But a Dom is merely a personality trait, sir. I didn't read anywhere in the manual where you can't be your own boss."

He stared at me in wide-eyed bafflement. "Wow. I mean you're right, of course, it is a personality trait." I braced for the *except* he clearly intended to voice. "But this is in regards to those in this lifestyle. The lifestyle you

18

clearly have no clue about. The lifestyle you're auditioning to become the image for. People in the BDSM community don't consider a Dom just someone who's her own boss. It's far more than being assertive or bossy."

"The ad described me. I'm a perfectly good Dom. People listen to me when I tell them what to do. I take charge. I get things done. If there's a problem, I solve it I don't whine and cry about it. I'm my own boss in my life, and I don't take shit. Or cry."

The grin he wore was on the edge of becoming rude. "Or cry."

I rolled my eyes. "If you have a point to make, sir, make it. I'm not into word games."

"Does this mean you're asking me to become your Dom?"

I stared at him, dumbfounded. "What?" And yet something in his demeanor called to me, insisting.

"Well, you called me sir…"

"Oh God," I muttered, pretending to go back to reading my Kindle. "Not that kind, the normal kind." I glanced at him. "And who is your Dom?"

He grinned, a look of pure joy. Like he was having the time of his life. "Nobody." The grin never faded with his answer.

"Oh so you can be your own Dom but I can't?"

"I'm a Dom over subs. You have subs?"

I shrugged a shoulder. "Are you available?"

"Oh fuck!" He literally *giggled*, like he couldn't believe his good fortune cookies.

I just wished I knew exactly what he found so very funny. "Is that a yes?"

"Do you want a sub to Dominate?"

Another serious question. I had to remember that this lifestyle was real to him. To all these people. It was a form of therapy for them, I reminded myself. And I really needed to practice playing along. "I dominate subs in the real world all day. Do I want or need someone to dominate sexually? No."

"Do *you* want to be dominated sexually?"

Survival instincts kicked down my adrenalin door at the combination of those words. Dominate and sex. "Not particularly."

"Not particularly."

20

"Let's go with not. Just not. No. I don't want to be dominated sexually. I don't want to be dominated in any way. I want to dominate. It's what I do, who I am. And I want to win this competition. That's why I'm here. This isn't a rush or high for me. I'm not a Domaholic, I'm just…" I swiped my kindle screen, trying to think of the right words.

"Domaholic?" His voice went all funny with amazement. "Fuck, you're so cute."

"Doesn't say you have to be for real. I can role play. I've read all about it." We moved slowly forward again.

"So you saw the ad for this competition and you thought, hey, I'm a natural Dom, I could win that."

I shrugged and nodded trying to think why that was clearly stupid. "Yes." I seriously couldn't find anything glaringly idiotic.

He dropped his head and shook it. "Do you have any idea what is going to be required of you in this competition, sweetheart?"

My stomach knotted at the dangerous warning in his words, tinged with sympathy. Again I managed nonchalance. "Not particularly. You?"

He studied me for several seconds before his face slowly went serious. "I'm not entirely sure to be honest. But could include things you wouldn't want to do."

"You sound so sure."

"I'm very sure."

I put my Kindle in my bag and leveled a professional stare at him only to realize immediately, he was *not* one of my clients. He met my gaze with a ferocity I wasn't used to. "I'm very sure you can't possibly be sure. Yes, you can look at me and make some assumptions, I get that."

He put his hand on my back and prompted me forward to close the gap in the moving line.

"And…well that doesn't mean you know me." I stepped out of the steaming hot touch of his hand. "I may be a little clumsy and I may not fit the picture you're used to seeing but don't let that fool you into thinking I'm not capable of accomplishing anything I set my mind to." I angled my body and viewed the progress in the line. "Moving right along now."

I finally chanced a peripheral glance his way and my heart raced at how he stared at me. Intimidation. That's all.

"If you respond to every simple touch like that, love, you're not going to make it past auditions. And I'm glad, really."

"I'm sure you are. That's one less challenge for you."

"Hardly. One less sweet angel about to get burned where the devils come to play."

Oh geeze. If only he didn't have that sincere tone, it'd make it a lot easier to play this game with him. But he wasn't playing. I gave an unladylike snort. "I'm no angel."

"Oh, God," he whispered, that fascination back.

"The fact that I'm doing this for money says I'm no angel." The stubborn streak in me insisted I prove to him how very un-angelic I could be.

"No it doesn't."

I swiveled my annoyed look to him. "And why are you harassing me again? Why should you care who comes to this audition? Who are you, an undercover moral policeman?" I added my sweet smile then. "Like it or not, I'm here. If they laugh me off the stage, what does it hurt you?"

"Good, God." He looked around. "Is your mother being held at gunpoint somewhere? Your child?" He looked at me, perplexity at its sexy finest. "I just can't believe you would do this. No, I don't know you, but think about how this looks to somebody, anybody. Some virgin from a small town coming to audition to be the top *Dom?*" He scrunched his shoulders and held them. "That's... fucking insane, am I right?"

I snapped my hand up. "Could you just leave me alone? Unless you're here to help me, I'd prefer you zip it." I dug my Kindle back out of my bag. "I'll just be reading if you don't mind."

"No, go ahead. Cram for your test, sweetheart." His tone mocked me, as if he humored a child, or a mentally challenged person.

"Why don't you do something useful and help me prepare? Since you're so interested in my sure failure."

Those broad shoulders expressed his amazement with a shrug. "I could kiss you."

My hormones train-wrecked until nothing but moronic syllables flooded my mind. Thankfully they didn't come out of my mouth. "I'm being serious. Please."

"Please..." His voice lowered to that soft sincerity I was beginning to recognize as his trademark. "So am I."

"Oh dear God, you are a piece of work. Where did you take classes to be that smooth?" I angled a smile and nodded. "You are really good."

"I am good." Like he stated simple fact.

"Ohhhh, I bet you are. Plenty of practice, eh?"

"Yes. That's what a Dom does."

"No, no, no, that's what *you* do. I don't recall reading where it said you *had* to take fifty women and…" I wavered my hand in the air, "do…private things with them."

"Use your BDSM vocabulary words." As if I were a toddler. "I spank them. Force them to orgasm over and over again. Worship their pussy. Their body. I bite them, fuck them hard and—"

"I get it! Jesus Christ." I wagged the Kindle at him. "It's all in here, I don't need you to recite the whole thing."

"Yes you do. I assure you, you do. There's no doubt going to be a written test and several physical ones."

Oh hell. "Physical? Like what?"

His grin bordered on sadistic. "Oh, I don't know. Something along the lines of demonstrating Dominance."

"They said nothing sexual." I hated how small my voice sounded.

"In the audition."

I pursed my lips mostly to keep from chewing them to shreds. "Oh." Yeah, I'd wondered what all might be involved *after* the audition. "I'm sure it won't be too over the top. I mean, it's going to be on television. They can't get too extreme."

He released an *oh shit* sound of incredulity. "Online, sweetheart. Pay Per View."

"So? Everything is online."

"Oh dear God," he whispered in awe of me. "This is online *because* it's so over the top, sweetheart."

I stared at him, mouth open like a fly-catcher. There was no hiding the oh-crap train wreck in my mind.

He nodded, no doubt seeing it. "But you haven't walked through those doors, love. You can turn around now, and go back to where you came from. After you give me your phone number."

Fear, insult, and intrigue ran circles in my gut at all he just said and meant. "I'm…" I looked around and took a deep breath with my eyes closed. I saw Gramma's face, her jaw trembling, eyes full of tears, the lines at her brow etched with the horror that gave me nightmares. And the orderly working there, the one I'd gone to high school with, who'd grown into a giant with a severely negative vibe. My resolved hardened. "I'm in. I'm doing it."

I met his gaze, surprised at the sadness I saw there. He stepped closer and I braced myself as his thumb glided over my cheek. The world disappeared as he held me with that damn…stuff in his eyes, too many things I wasn't familiar with.

"Whatever it is, it's not worth it. I don't know what's going on but please, don't do this."

I waved off the fear he produced. "I'll be fine. They can't like kill me or anything, right?" I laugh/snorted a little. "Okay, you're freaking me out with that look."

"No, they can't kill you, love."

I fanned my face at the unspoken things in his tone. "I'll tell you what." Past time to lighten the mood. "How about we make a little deal." I landed my hand on his shoulder for a truce. "You help me through this and… I'll split the winnings with you if I win."

I held my breath as he stepped right up to me and put his warm hands on either side of my face in the softest caress. Surely he wouldn't... oh dear. His lips lowered to mine then paused just before touch down. "I'll do it." He placed a feather soft kiss on the edge of my mouth and pulled up, his gaze sending sparks through my body at warp speed. "In fact..." he smiled barely with that relentless gaze, "...I'd *pay you* to let me."

"Ha." The crazy sounding laugh came with my incessant nods. I couldn't seem to make them stop as I looked around. "Okay."

"What's your name, by the way?"

"Oh! Tara. Tara Reese."

"Lucian Bane." He held his hand out to me and I shook it.

"Guess it's a good idea to know the name of the person you're..." Ah, shit. I drew my hand back and looked around. "Line's moving."

Chapter Three

Tara. It wasn't just her name that rubbed my cock the wrong way, it was that she was a clueless woman running against me for the Ultimate Dom position. So unfair for her. My heart stopped as she emerged from the bathroom in black heels and dress. I watched as she bent to drink from the water fountain, my eyes landing on the perfect curve of her ass. Stomping grounds had never looked so enticing, that was for damn sure.

She straightened and looked around. She spotted me and walked over, her stride oddly confident in this outfit. She was really going through with it. Every moment that passed, I kept expecting her to back out, to turn and run her lovely ass back to her car. But she stayed. Fine. If I couldn't talk her into quitting, maybe I could make sure she lost. Now that they'd officially signed us up as a pair, it should be pretty simple. Some day she might even thank me for it.

Things moved more quickly now that we'd made it past the written test. That phase had eliminated roughly half of the competition in short order. They'd moved the remaining contestants into a room that resembled a small cinema to await the next phase. An outraged grumble had passed through the group when the pair requirement was announced. One male bitched about the big coincidence that equal numbers of males and females had advanced. He was wrong on that, though. I'd spotted several male/male pairs.

A gruff voice up near the front of the room sounded familiar and I searched for the speaker. Oh God. No way that bastard still walked the streets a free man.

A burly dude rose and turned to someone behind him. "And I'll say it again. Every so-called Dom here will sub to me." A cruel mouth twisted into a sneer.

"There's no competition. They should have just called me to start with. If they'd talked to anyone really in the lifestyle, they'd have known that."

My muscles tightened with the urge to leap over the rows of seats and shut the bastard's mouth. The attitude certainly hadn't changed since I'd last encountered Jase

Duff. The intervening years melted away and suddenly I was eight years younger, sitting in the public room of Mistress Stacia's Playroom. It was the biggest BDSM club in the Dallas-Fort Worth area and had a formidable reputation for strict enforcement of the rules.

Silence fell in the public room as two of the male subs carefully supported a female between them. Even with their help, the girl barely stayed upright. A lurid bruise puffed her cheekbone and blood trickled from the corner of her mouth. Legs bared by her mini skirt were covered with welts that oozed blood.

Master Duff turned back to his subs. "Let her go. She refused the care and protection of my collar. She can find her own way out." He turned on his heel and strode to the door.

The male subs glanced to one another, then gently lowered the young woman to the floor. Faces carefully neutral, they followed their Master.

I looked around, furious that nobody seemed inclined to help the girl. "You can't just leave her. She needs care."

Everyone in the room held their breath as Master Duff froze. "Boy, I don't know who you are and I don't care. I'm going to give you the benefit of the doubt, since you obviously are ignorant of certain expectations. No one challenges a Master unless they are prepared for the consequences."

I glanced around to find every single face turned away from me. They might not like Duff, but they didn't feel strongly enough about it to challenge him, even as a group. "No decent master would leave her in that condition."

"What's going on here?" A feminine voice cut through the tension. Mistress Stacia strode into the room, black leather corset gleaming against smooth ivory skin. The tip of her riding crop snapped against the delicate-looking embossed leather that snugly covered her calf.

One of her own subs came forward to explain in hushed tones. As he spoke, she looked from the Master to the poor girl still on the floor. "Master Duff, I've told you before not to cross my lines. This does. Harming a sub to the point they need medical attention serves none of us. We're allowed to exist because we don't draw attention from the vanilla world. Henceforth, my Playroom shall be relieved of your patronage." She turned toward the injured girl. "Take her to my private rooms."

He didn't show up in my life again for a while, but when he did, he made a point to remind me who he was. His victim that night had become my first collared sub, and he was not happy about that either. Thus far, I'd always managed to elude his little revenge fantasies by outsmarting him.

He would be fucking trouble.

Beside me, Tara stirred in her seat, shifting her e-reader around to a more comfortable position. Squirming a little, she leaned her mouth close to my ear. "Who's the loudmouth?"

Duff was still going on about how lame he considered the competition.

I had to make sure Tara didn't pop up on his radar. If he so much as saw her sitting with me, a bull's-eye would appear on her forehead. "He's a serious loser. I can't believe he's still walking the streets."

She stared skeptically at Duff. "He doesn't look that scary."

"You're judging him by vanilla standards. Imagine a guy with cruel tendencies, only none of the normal rules apply to him. He can do whatever he wants and no one will stop him. That's Jase Duff."

An almost speculative look crossed her face. "Listen to me Tara." I took her hand to make sure I had her full attention. She faced me, one brow lifted slightly. "If you go anywhere near that bastard, I walk. You'll lose."

The eyebrow went up a bit further. "Oh. You think I can't do this without you?"

Caution made me back off a little. "Let's just say you go near him, I'll make sure you lose. One way or another."

Finally, the tall blonde announcer stood at the front again. The room went quiet waiting for her to call the next pair. "Lucian Bane. Tara Reese."

I stood and drew Tara with me and the blonde's sharp gaze zeroed in on us.

"This way." She waited for us to catch up and showed us through the door at the side. We followed down a broad corridor until she stopped outside a metal door. "You'll find a description of your task inside. You have fifteen minutes to strategize, then you'll be taken in front of the committee." She waited until we were inside the little room and closed the door behind us.

A sealed envelope imprinted with our names sat on the little cheap-looking side table crowded between a pair of stained office chairs. Tara flew over and ripped open the envelope then sat in the chair, mumbling through the words.

I finally made out what we were supposed to do even though she wasn't sure and re-read it. They wanted the Dom to make first contact with a potential sub.

I dropped into the other chair and she suddenly looked up at me, a little puzzled. I spelled it out simply, "They want us to pretend we're just meeting and see how well I can pick up a new sub."

"You?"

"Unless you have experience picking up subs besides 'hi, my name is Tara, I'm an adorable sexy woman who would like to have intercourse with you'. If we're going to win, I'm playing Dom."

The pulse fluttering at the base of her throat caught my attention, beckoning. Her nervousness set my instincts into overdrive and I had to push back the urge to soothe her. If she were going to play sub, letting her be frightened and ignorant of what I would do was good. "Just follow my lead."

Whatever reason had induced Tara to audition, must have entered her mind, because she suddenly became that woman willing to put her own self aside and do what it took to get the job done. Even if it meant listening to me. Thankfully.

"Okay. I'll follow your lead. Should we practice?"

I took a slow breath, staring at her, mentally going over what I'd do until adrenalin and the need to do it hummed inside me. "It'll be more authentic if you don't know."

"Are you sure?"

Fuck, that fragile thing in her voice that was so at odds with her personality, tickled my Dom urges. I wanted to pin her in a corner, shove her dress up and force her to orgasm where she stood. "I'm sure, love."

"If you're sure then."

She wanted another affirmation but I closed my eyes and let my head rest against the wall behind the chair. I needed to think of the best way to proceed.

The moments passed and Tara, like a very good little sub, didn't interrupt my thoughts. A sharp tap at the door was our only warning when the blonde came to escort us to the audition. We followed her down a hall until she stopped outside another door.

"This leads to the staging area. Once you enter, you have sixty seconds to get into position. The lights will go up and you are to start your act then. You'll have ten minutes, then the bell will ring, signaling your time is up." She opened the door and nodded for us to go through.

I touched Tara's hand. "Remember, follow my lead."

She nodded and moved into the room. Glancing back to me, I nodded that she was doing the right thing as she went to the little bar they'd brought in, complete with a stool, and took a seat.

I waited at a short distance, keeping my gaze pinned to Tara, encouraging her with sheer will power.

The blonde called out, "In three, two, one." The lights went up.

I took my time, allowing my vision to adjust to the glare. Not exactly club atmosphere. I strolled forward, looking around, as if seeking someone. Approaching the bar, I was impressed with Tara's instincts to do just as she might in real life. Not look.

I stopped behind her and waited a few heartbeats. "Hello."

She angled her head at me and I locked my gaze on hers, pretending we were alone, and this was me, doing what I would do if I'd met her someplace else. I allowed myself to know as much about her as I did, which was only enough to make me hungry, very hungry to know all. "I'm Lucian."

She turned to me in that confidence, her gaze saying *make me. Break me if you can.* Then she stood and stumbled slightly in her heels. Her courage faltered and that brief vulnerability shot desire through my bones and flooded me with reckless needs to tear into her body, mark her so hard and deep that she had to be mine.

My arm shot out to steady her and she jerked her gaze up, the look in her eyes screaming, *Oh God, I'm ruining it.*

"I got you," I soothed in whisper.

Her head angled toward the judges and I reached with a finger and turned her face to me. "Just me. Only see me. Now, listen. Are you listening, love?"

She gave a barely nod.

"Good. Because I have something important to say to you." I tipped her chin up with one finger and dipped to bring my mouth to hers.

Right on cue, she turned slightly so that my kiss found the corner of her mouth. I moved closer, and she stepped back, which put her against the bar.

Tara's breathing quickened when she could go no further. All her doubts were visible in her eyes. What had she gotten herself into?

Her innocence was brutal and there was something about it, something different that turned my Dom into a prowling wolf. I slid my hand along her neck, slowly. Panic turned her head, but I held her jaw still, watching her fight the instinct to bail. The mix of her submissiveness and innocence was nearly overwhelming my own control. My fingers pressed harder into her jaw with unmistakable intention that made her gasp. I lowered and took the kiss I had to have but it wasn't the one she was expecting. I slid my lips gently across hers.

"I just want to protect you." I nibbled at her mouth, enticing her trust. She didn't attempt to stop me, and even parted her lips a little. The little gift fucking slammed me with desire. But, topping for me wasn't forcing, it was fair persuasion. I deepened the kiss and she gifted me again with submission. And given who she was, what that cost her, what it meant to her, made the gift all the more precious.

I realized in that second, the tables had turned on me. Need drove my dominance to have unthinkable things. I wanted what was buried far beneath that lovely skin of hers, beneath that strict disciplined will. I wanted beyond that protective wall inside her, that place she didn't allow anybody, not even herself.

I slid my hand to the back of her head and into her hair, tangling the spun silk around my fingers. Her eyes flew wide with a small cry that sent my pulse racing.

My hold kept her head back and her body arched against me in attempt to remain upright. Fear flashed in her eyes and I stifled her whimpers with more soft kisses. "I got you baby. Don't panic, I'm not going to hurt you."

She latched onto my shoulders to keep from falling. Perfect.

I kissed my way along her jaw until my mouth was at her ear. "You're doing beautifully sweetheart. Please trust me." Tremors passed from her body into mine and I soothed them with a firm hand along her spine. "Shhh." My hand glided lower over her ass and muscular upper thigh. "Sweetheart, you're fucking beautiful, do you know that?"

She gave a whimper in my ear as I lifted her leg up, sliding it decisively along mine before pulling her into my raging erection.

Panic clicked her frigid button and I moved to her lips and let my desire loose. With a hunger I didn't have to pretend, I held her jaw firmly and pushed her lips open with mine. I stroked her tongue with irrefutable passion, allowing my dominance to guide me for the final countdown. She submitted to my dominance until the tension in her body became eager.

Her hands ran up into my hair and she returned the kiss. The sensation blasted me with hunger and my threadbare control vanished. We suddenly struggled to get closer, deeper, more, faster.

"Lucian."

The soft whimper of my name came with a bucket of ice water in the form of a bell.

"Thank you," a voice called out, signaling we could leave.

I took Tara's hand and led her carefully from the stage. She could barely walk without tripping every other step. The poor baby needed aftercare from a mere kiss.

And I needed to hear her say my name again just like she had. The things that did to me were unthinkable. Unbearable. Unexplainable. Many women had called my name, and I'd liked it, loved it. But when she called it, it spoke to me in another way. No, it called to me. Wrong again. It called to *somebody else* in me.

Chapter Four

I paced up and down in the room, hardly able to believe we'd actually made it to the final round. Five couples would compete to win now.

I really shouldn't go check on her again, but Jase Duff had made it to the next level too, and the way he eyed her made me feel antsy. He was one very sick puppy. And there were no cameras in the personal rooms.

Duff played by the rules but just barely, and only when he thought someone was looking. He was like the step-father that only *nearly* killed you, the killer that made you wish he'd just get it over with already. The others were like kittens compared to him even though they were still threats.

I sat on the bed and threw myself onto it, covering my face with both hands. What was Tara doing? How scared was she?

I sat up, recalling her response to my kiss. Mother-fuck, I'd been worried about her reaction. We aced the audition because the truth was, neither of us were pretending. I'd meant every word, she'd meant every response.

I groaned at the fierce throb in my cock, remembering those sounds and the way she tried not to make them but couldn't contain it. The way her breath trembled with her body. The way she held on to my neck because she'd lost strength in her legs. But there was so much resistance in that body of hers, every muscle was lined tight with it. Made me want to fucking crush it.

And to think I would get to spend three days exploring her. Fuck, had I died and gone to heaven? She wasn't a sub, not at all. That was the dynamic. She was this…this woman, this strange and amazing woman, this puzzle I needed to sit and stare at and piece together. And I would. For the next three days, I'd piece her together.

After I tore her completely apart.

****

"Oh dear God oh dear God, oh dear God." I paced up and down in my room shaking my hands. I dropped to the floor and began doing crunches. Just needed to work

44

out this energy. I'd made it. Made it through the audition. Thanks to Lucian.

Memories of his lips flooded my body with heat and I picked up speed. Fifty-two, fifty-three. The next thing I knew, the rasp of his tongue heated my neck again. Sixty-four, sixty-five. My privates throbbed in memory of his hard fingers biting into my leg and pulling me into his gorgeous body. Oh Jesus, he'd been *aroused. A lot!* Forty-five, forty…

I gave up and lay there, panting and winded as the memory continued to consume me. I'd never been kissed that way. So that was dominance? Wasn't so bad. I could handle that kind of stuff.

I looked for the packet I was supposed to read through. The rules to the game that we had to figure out on our own. As adults.

Thirty minutes later, I sat on the edge of the bed with the rule book in my hand, astounded with adrenalin, fear, and desire at imagining what was coming. Every day we had to pick from a list of activities. Each one was worth points. We could mix them as we liked, but each activity was only worth points one time. We could repeat things, but points would only be awarded the first time.

Some of the activities I'd never be able to do. Sex being one. Both the literal and oral. Could I... maybe do him orally? Maybe. There were plenty of small point items I could do, spooning being the easiest of all. We were allowed to drink, so maybe I could get drunk and wipe that whole list out. Regret later. But then we both had to do things from the list. How was I supposed to get him to not do certain things?

Money. I'd pay him money.

Oh God. But then we wouldn't hardly make any points. We had to do some of it. I flew up and paced, chewing my thumb nail, going through that list again. I could do the sadistic things maybe. I could ask him to as well. It was just pain. I could handle that. Yeah, that could work.

I rushed to the little night stand and pulled out my journal and pen. I opened the rule book and began marking things. N for *no way*. M for *maybe*. Y for *yes*. I added the points for the *yeses* and *maybes*. Then I added the points for the *no ways*.

My heart sank. The *no ways* topped both by a hundred and fifty. And judging by the competition, they'd be racking up.

I regarded the *yeses* and *maybes*. If we mixed them we might be able to make it. I could definitely kiss him. Could I do the nude thing? Dear God, the idea of walking around him nude was unthinkable. Keep that one in the *maybe* list. For now. I began working various scenarios to see how many points we could make. Oh wow. If he collared me, and led me like a dog, *while* I was nude, that was thirty points. I could let him tie me up and blindfold me and cut on me a little.

That would definitely rack up points. But that still left out what *he* had to do. I'd deal with him when the time came.

Chapter Five

I followed behind Tara to the room we'd be sharing.

The Dungeon Manager opened our door and turned. "Remember the rooms have cameras everywhere, even in the closets."

I followed Tara in, anxious to see how she was holding up. She hadn't even looked at me since we'd met up in the hallway.

"Welcome to your domain." The curvaceous female Dom Manager opened both arms wide. The movement separated the front of her jacket, which would have been perfectly appropriate in the boardroom, to reveal an intricate leather and lace corset. "This is the living room, obviously."

We continued to follow the perfectly straight seam at the back of her silk stockings through an arched entry into a large kitchen. "Your kitchen. It's stocked with food and drinks. It's like having your very own bar." She smiled and opened a cabinet that held every kind of liquor before spinning and leading us back through the archway.

I watched Tara who still hadn't given me any indication of her wellbeing. A tiny smile was all I needed.

"This is the bedroom with attached glamour bath. Plenty of fun to be had here. The bathroom is stocked, first aid kit included." She giggled as she walked to the other side of the room and threw open French doors. "And your mini-dungeon." She stepped aside.

I watched Tara's reaction to the room loaded neatly full of toys, ready for action. I bit my lower lip to keep from grinning at the shameless gawk she wore.

"Impressive, huh?" the woman said.

Tara finally leveled a you've *got to be kidding me* look.

"Okay, I'll leave you two love birds to the task." She turned and headed out then paused. "Everything is in the rule books. And don't forget. One of you quits, you're both disqualified." She flashed a flawless smile, her eyes lingering on me longer than necessary. "If you have an emergency, use the phone."

We followed her back to the main exit where again she paused, this time her eyes on Tara. "I hope you know what to do with him baby. Because I sure would." She winked at me and smiled at Tara. "Go team Lucian."

The door shut and Tara mocked, "Go team Lucian," in a midget voice.

I bit back a grin. "Wow."

She looked at me, annoyance in her pretty hazel eyes. "What? Wow what?"

"Just you barely know me and you're jealous. I love that."

"Pffft! As if! Jealous." She locked the door and spun to the living room with her bag. "Did you bring your rule book? I hope so because I marked mine all up."

"I did." I pulled the rolled up book from my back pocket and wagged it at her.

She stared at me for a few seconds. "Have you read it?"

"Of course."

"Well, what did you get out of it? I got that the first day we play sub and Dom. The second day there's some kind of community activity." She had an *ick* look on her face. "And the third day…"

"Sub and Dom again," I helped.

"Yes, that." She opened up her book and I made my way over, noticing how frayed her pages were.

"What'd you do, bathe with it?"

"I read it. A lot. Studied it." She regarded me. "And what did you do with yours? I hope you gave some thought about getting us major points."

I sat back with a laugh. "Yeah, I did. All night long. How are you holding up?"

"Fine." She pulled out her little pen and tapped it on her blue jeaned knee.

"So." I regarded the curve of her ass where it met the couch. "Who is going to be Dom and who is going to be sub today?"

"I was thinking I should be Dom."

I nodded. "Kinda figured that."

"Well you know I'm not good sub material. At least let me warm up."

"I don't know love, you rocked that audition as a sub."

She cleared her throat, obviously not liking the reminder. "I was nervous."

"That you were." I left it at that, my tongue restless to say so much more. "Fine, ladies first. You can be the Dom. I'll be the sub."

She looked over her shoulder. "You can handle that?"

My cock got hard at hearing she might actually care. "I'm sure I can handle being topped by you, baby."

"Don't call me that."

"Okay. Would you like me to call you? Master? Or Sir? MaDom?"

She rolled her eyes.

"It has to be authentic, love."

"Don't call me that either."

"Okay sweetheart."

"Tara! My name is Tara. And fine. Sir. Call me sir."

"Sir Tara."

"God that's so *stupid*."

"Master Tara?"

"Call me Tara. That's what you call me. I'm the Dom, you're the sub. I can make whatever rules up I want."

I smiled, impressed. "Very good." She was catching on. "I'm at your service Tara."

"Well let's get started." She handed me a worked over paper.

I looked at it and marveled that I was actually turned on with her messy handwriting. I'd waited too fucking long to get laid, that was my problem.

She recited her list. "Collar me. Lead me like a dog. Maximum allowed cuts on my arms as shallow as you can please."

I shook my head.

"What?" She looked dumbfounded. "I'm the Dom, you can't say no."

"You have it all wrong, sweetheart. As the Dom, you collar *me*, lead *me* like a dog, cut *me*."

"Oh." Her face fell as she realigned all the rules in that lovely head. Suddenly she brightened. "But I'm the *Dom*! You do as I say. I can like those things even as a Dom, and you have to do them."

I couldn't argue there. It may not have been standard practice, but everybody was allowed their kink, whatever it was. "Okay, we *might* get by with that." I went on. "Cook you a meal. Feed you. And clean up." I lowered the paper and regarded her. "Those are the kinds of things a sub does for the Dom."

She gave me a look that said he was being dense. "I'm the Dom. This Dom likes to do sub things." She went to pacing next to the couch. "Anyway, that should take care of the first hour. I calculated it."

"And what will you be doing next? Sleeping in the cage?"

She looked at me, serious. "How many points is that?"

"Tara, the sub sleeps in the cage." I sighed and got the rule book. "And it's a whopping five points."

"What?!" She snatched the book from me and looked. "Five! For sleeping like an animal in a cage?" She let out a disgusted noise. "Oh look, fifty for self-gratification, because that's so much more… dominating. Who makes this up, anyway?"

"While you whine and complain, I'll go fetch our toys." I got up and went to the playroom and looked through the selection. I picked the white silk blindfold and matching collar. She would look good in white silk. I slid my gaze over all the toys, energy racing through me at what was eventually coming. Me. Her.

I returned to find her pacing along the couch. She stopped and faced me. "Change of plans. You. Forced Masturbation first, then the rest. Can you handle that?" She stared at the invisible person next to me.

I dared not rock the love boat by asking why the change of plans. "Will you be watching me?"

"Uh?" She held up the blindfold in answer.

"Yeah. Well, don't be so sure you'll get the points for it if you're not watching."

She pursed those sexy lips, thinking. "I'm willing to take my chances. It could be considered demeaning. Like where the sub does crap and the Dom is *aloof*." She didn't hide how stupid she thought that was and I didn't hide how cute I thought she was.

"Fine. Forced Masturbation while you're *aloof* it is." I began undoing my pants.

"Blindfold me!" She spun and presented her back.

I tied the blindfold on and turned her toward me. "Where would you like me to stroke my cock until I come, love?"

I smiled at how her jaw dropped then snapped back shut. "You can...do you need to do it in the bathroom?"

"Where do you want me?"

She swallowed. "I'd like you to do it in the bathroom."

"Would you consider performing mutual self-gratification? It would double our score."

"No, no no no."

"Can I do it here? On the couch?"

"Why?"

"Well, I happen to have a hard time with the task."

She cocked her head a little. "As in... what."

"As in I can't complete the job."

She sighed and let her head fall back in a groan. "And here would help that?"

I stared at the white column of her neck. "I need to see you."

"What?" she nearly squeaked. "What about one of the-the magazines I saw in there?"

"I don't want to look at porn, thank you."

"Well it's not about what you want. It's about submitting to what I say."

I bit my tongue in frustration. "Okay but I still may not be able to."

"Why?"

"Because porn just doesn't do it for me, Tara."

"Once you start—"

"I think I know my own fucking body to know what I can and can't do. I'm burnt out on porn, okay, I've had my fill. I don't want to see it, I don't want to jack off to it."

She almost appeared momentarily impressed before she crossed her arms over her chest. "I'm not getting undressed."

This was getting annoying. "You don't need to. But I'll be getting comfortable."

"Okay then. Fine. As long as I don't have to look."

I stood there feeling like I'd just won the right to dip my cock in hot glue. I removed my clothes and sat on the couch then stared up at her.

She turned toward me a bit. "Are you..."

"Haven't started, love."

"How long does it—"

"Holy, fuck. An hour at this rate."

"Okay, okay." Her words were softer. "What… can I do?"

My heart throbbed as hard as my cock. "Sit next to me."

She reached behind her, feeling for the couch then sat erectly on the edge. "This good enough?"

God, no. "Yes." I stared at her mouth, remembering what it felt like under my dominance, remembering everything about that kiss and what it had done to me.

"God, people are watching this."

The shame in her voice was foreign to me. I'd grown used to group orgies. Having another pair of eyes or a million didn't matter. I stroked my hand up and down my cock, wishing she didn't have on that bulky t-shirt. "I need to see you."

She turned a little toward me.

"I mean you. Your body." My voice strained a little as I stroked my cock, my hard-on beyond raging now with her sitting there.

"Geeze," she said, distressed. "How much?"

"Take your shirt off. That's all."

She made frustrated sounds of hesitation.

"You have a bra on." It was a wager, but I'd have bet a million dollars on it. And that she wore boy cut underwear.

"I know but..." She quickly removed her shirt and crossed her arms over her chest. "It's not like there's a lot to see."

"Fuck," I gasped, heat filling my balls. Not much to see. She had a B cup. Black lace bra. Small breasts were my fucking weakness. There was something about them, maybe the inadequacy they always seemed to come with. It did something for my dominant nature. "Hold my hand. I have to touch you."

She didn't move and I stroked long and slow along my cock, slick with my pre-cum. I imagined it was her mouth moving up and down it. She finally reached slowly toward me and I laced my fingers in hers.

"Your breasts are perfect, love." Another wager I was ready to bet a million on. I gasped and moaned with my approaching orgasm. I'd never have dreamed just holding a person's hand could be such a turn on. "Fuck." The whisper came with a groan.

"Is it... is it working?"

The breathless desire in her voice did it. I gripped her hand tight and thrust my hips, watching her still face. Even with the blindfold on, I could see it, her desire. No, it wasn't just desire with her, it was something much more potent than I'd ever seen. That I wanted to see more of. A lot more of. And hear. God, I needed to hear it. Feel it against my mouth. "Tara." Her name came on my final groan as the white hot took me. I wanted to fucking pull her to me, hold her, feel her. What a torture.

"Is it…over?"

I let out a choked gasp and sat there looking at her. "Yes."

She quickly untangled her hand from mine and worked her t-shirt back on. "Keep track of our points. Write it." She pointed toward the table, adjusting her blindfold.

"Can I clean myself off first?"

"Ew. Yes. Please do."

Okay, that wasn't nice. "Stop acting like a virgin."

She gave that snort. "This is not a virgin act. This is an ew, a stranger jacked off next to me while I was blindfolded act."

"Hey, you picked it."

"I wanted you to do it in the bathroom."

"And I couldn't." I picked up my t-shirt and wiped off.

"Yes, fault yours, not mine."

I shook my head and stood. "Can I lead you like a dog now? That would be great."

"Ha, ha. Yes, to the kitchen." She held out a hand like she were a queen. "Where you cook for me."

"I guess you want me to stay nude?"

"As long as I'm blindfolded, yes."

I got the collar ready. "Clever. I have to give you that."

****

"Lift your hair. Putting on your collar."

She lifted the shoulder length hair that reminded me of burnt toffee. I put the collar on her and tightened it to a caress then grabbed the leash and yanked a little in a downward direction. She got on her hands and knees and I led her to the high-end gourmet kitchen. "Aren't you just an adorable puppy?"

"Shut up."

I smiled. "You're at the table. What would you like to eat?"

"What can you cook?" She felt her way into a spindle backed maple chair.

"Anything."

"Oh, impressive. The quickest thing. Scrambled eggs."

"Coming right up. Tara."

I brought the plate of eggs over and sat across from her. "Open."

She kept her hands flat on the table. "You sound angry."

"So?"

She sat there for a few seconds. "Why?"

"Why does it matter?"

"It doesn't. Well... I don't want you to be mad at me."

I stared at her, all my need from earlier rushing back in. "I'm not mad," I said softer. Just horny out of my fucking mind. "Now, open."

She complied and I carefully put the food in her mouth, watching her eat. "Wow, not bad." She angled her head up at the camera. "Extra points for amazing cook." I fed her another bite and the mmmm sounds she made as she chewed had me hard again in no time.

I placed the last of the food on her tongue, torturing myself. "You were hungry."

"Mmm, I guess I was."

"Would you like a drink?"

She continued making cock tickling noises. "Milk if they have it."

Milk. I liked the child-like choice. Did I like her soft side or what? More like loved it. I wanted to lick her all over. Slowly.

"I guess I'll clean and then you can take your blindfold off and come up with more of these amazing point combos."

"Hey! I'm doing the best with what I have." She angled her head like a blind person seeing with their ears. "Can you make coffee?"

Coffee. Milk. No alcohol yet. "You're tired already?"

"The blindfold is making me keep my eyes closed and yes, I'm tired. I too stayed awake all night."

"Not for the same reasons I did, I'll bet. Oh I almost forgot. I still need to cut you. We'll consider it dessert." I walked up to her and slid the blindfold off.

"Wh—" She stared at my naked body her protest frozen on her tongue. I realized she'd not seen it yet. And fuck her reaction wasn't helping my growing need to dominate her.

"Do you find me acceptable?"

She jerked her gaze up. "What?"

"My body."

She pffed and did that snort thing with a little wave of her hand. "It's just a... body. Everybody has one."

The obvious lie made me that much harder. Why did she affect me that way?

She gave a sudden painful sounding hiss. "Shoot. Let's get this cutting thing over with."

I finished the cleanup in the kitchen and lifted her leash. The urge to pet and stroke her was difficult to deny. "Let me lead you to the couch while I get what I'll need."

"Can I play a vicious dog and bite your ankle?"

I smiled. "I like biting."

"Oh yeah." She plodded along the wood floors. "I forgot you're weird."

"Don't knock it if you haven't tried it."

After getting her settled safely on the couch, I retrieved a sterile razor blade from the kit in the closet, along with alcohol swabs, gloves, and gauze. A fluffy white towel came from the bathroom.

I returned to find her perched nervously on the edge of the white leather loveseat. She looked up as I approached and her lips parted at being met once again, with my nudity like a shock she'd never get used to. Her gaze clung to my hard-on like a physical caress.

I didn't hide from her even though she was clearly not comfortable being with a naked man in any way. I made a point to sit close to her, placing the supplies on the coffee table, then laid the towel across my thigh. I left my hard-on exposed to give her something besides the razor blade to focus on. "Stretch your arm out, rest your hand here." I patted the towel. I prepared the supplies and even used the rubber glove for safety's sake.

She slowly complied, keeping her hand as far from my groin as possible. "Is this going to hurt?" Her tongue swept nervously over her lip.

"I'm cutting you with a blade, love." For the first time, I almost understood how the act of Blood Letting could be erotic for some.

Her cheeks were flushed, lips parted and her breathing accelerated. "But I mean… never mind just do it. Shallow." She bit her lip.

Need to soothe away her fears hit me like a runaway train. And still, I couldn't resist teasing. "I'll try."

Her eyes widened. "Try?"

"I'm kidding sweetheart." I couldn't hold back a chuckle.

"You're not supposed to call me that," she squeaked, bracing herself as I held her arm in a firm grip.

The smell of the alcohol swab permeated the air as I disinfected the silken skin of her inner forearm. I bent to blow gently, drying the dampness. I inspected her flawless skin, selecting the best places to make my cuts.

Her taut muscles vibrated with nervous anticipation and I couldn't keep from stroking her outer arm to alleviate some of her worry. "Ready?" My whisper made her jump a little. "I got you."

She squeezed her eyes tightly shut. "Just do it!" She held her breath.

I quickly drew the blade across her skin, careful to keep the cut shallow. A thin line of crimson welled in the little half inch long cut. I repeated the move four more times in quick succession. It was over before she knew it. "Open your eyes."

Her mouth flew open when she saw the little parallel lines of blood on her forearm. She squealed and danced her feet with a grimace while my stomach turned over. "Why didn't it hurt until now?" She squealed again. "Oh God, how bad is it?"

I gently pressed a square of gauze to the cuts. "They're hardly bleeding, sweetheart. Like a cat scratch." I kept hold of her arm, loving the size difference and the silky feel of her forearm skin. The towel over my thigh had slipped with all her dancing about, leaving her arm to rest on my bare skin.

Causing her real pain, even the slight burn of a razor blade cut, wasn't something I cared to repeat. Even my cock knew the difference between that sort of pain and the kind that enhanced sexual stimulation. It wasn't interested in cutting her either, and had gone soft with the first bite of the blade into her flesh.

"Okay, so we're done?"

I wiped more blood from her arm. "Aftercare."

"What?" She blinked as if she'd never encountered the term before.

"Rules for after play. Look it up."

I... I remember. Reading that. I mean, I believe you." She looked at her arm again, seeming almost shocked when fresh blood flowed to the surface. "So how do we do this after care crap and is it worth points?"

I took the collar off her and pulled her by the hand to the bathroom. "No. I just tend to you however you need."

"I don't need, so can we skip?"

"No, you can't. Getting an infection in your cuts would be a stupid move, don't you think?"

She nodded a little while dabbing at the gauze. "True."

I found antibiotic ointment and bandages in the first aid kit and put them on the wide double vanity, then patted the counter. Her ass didn't quite reach so I lifted her up to sit between the twin basins.

Before she could feel awkward about a naked man standing between her knees, I held her outstretched arm and applied the ointment. "So what do you have in mind next?"

"Um. It's… on my list."

"Ah." I opened the first bandage and covered the scratch. "Are you having fun yet?"

She gave me a smile that made me want to walk her out of this fucking world. And into my apartment. "Eh. It's not so bad. Could be worse."

I snuck another glance at her and caught her staring at my chest. Then she raised her gaze and sledge hammered me with desire. Obeying the hunger in her eyes, I leaned in to kiss her only to have her lean away and out of reach.

Right. I was the only one willing to indulge her appetites. Not her. Yet. She'd get there.

I finished bandaging her cuts then helped her down.

As soon as her feet hit the floor, she promptly hurried back to the living room and I followed, need making every muscle in my body ache. She passed me, heading back toward the bedroom. No, the *play* room. I followed, curious. She had her little strategy paper out, and for some reason, I found that fucking adorable. Ought to be interesting.

She glared warily at the neatly organized toys like one might a nest of spiders, clutching the worn paper to her chest. "Which one is a flogger?"

I went to the right wall. "This." One by one, I touched the other types of floggers. "And this. And that."

"Oh, variety. With different points." She walked a little closer and reached only a finger toward the one worth fifty. The thin leather cords of the lashes were tipped with small metal beads "Wonder why that one is so much? Because it hurts worse?"

"Uh. Yeah."

She backed up and scanned the walls of horror. She pointed to a series of metal rings joined by a leather strap. "What's that?"

"Gates of Hell."

She made a hissing sound. "I remember reading about it." She gave me a speculative look, scanning my body. Every time she did that, desire colored her cheeks. Only she wasn't aware of it. "Have you done that?"

"God, no." I shuddered at the thought.

"Which ones have you done? I need something easy." Her gaze lowered to my torso again, like she couldn't help herself. How long would I be able to stand this? She wasn't teasing. Not intentionally anyway, but the monster inside didn't bother to make the distinction of innocence.

"All the toys I like are for women. But spankings are worth twenty-five points each. And I'd even close my eyes." Anything to touch her flesh, her ass especially. "Though as the Dom, you really should be the one spanking me." I inserted a wistful note in my voice.

She worried at her full bottom lip then snapped her fingers. "No. You spank me. I'll blindfold you for extra points." She hurried back to the living room and I followed, triumph roaring through my blood.

She got the blindfold from the kitchen table and returned, indicating for me to let her put it on. I turned and she gasped. "I can collar you too! What am I thinking? You need to help come up with things."

"Sweetheart, if you let me, we'd accumulate more points than you could imagine."

"I'm sure you could, but I prefer the clean strategy." She buckled the leather collar loosely around my neck.

"And as your sub, I am obliged to let you." I left the unspoken warning of what was coming when I was Dom. "Make it a little tighter?"

"Really?" She adjusted the buckle until I nodded. "I think we're doing fine." The cute pout in her voice turned my Dom into a mewling pussy cat wanting to lick boo boos.

"Well, we'll know this evening."

She let out a sigh that sounded as if she were half-resigned to some unpleasant fate. "Okay now what?"

"Lead me to the couch."

"Might as well crawl while we're at it, might give us more points."

I dropped to all fours, following obediently when she gave the leash an experimental tug. "Aww aren't you such a cute puppy?"

"You might not say that in a minute." My hands tingled with anticipation and my cock throbbed as visions of rubbing my cum into the red marks I'd put on her ass added to my torment.

"Oh please." The tone of her voice gave away her broad grin and eye roll. "I think I can handle a spanking. You're at the couch."

I fumbled around for her foot and she took my hand and helped me up. I allowed the head of my hard-on to brush against her. She jumped as if she'd been burned, but stayed silent while guiding me to sit.

"How do you want to do this?" Her voice quivered a little, but she gave no other indications of worry.

Temptation surged through me, urging outrageous demands. Barely managing, I held out my hand for her. "Over my lap."

She didn't take my hand but she did lay on my lap. The denim of her jeans felt rough against my thighs. Not the silky skin I'd anticipated. "Sweetheart. This is B.D. S. M. You remember what that stands for? You remember where you are, what you're doing? Take the clothes off."

"What? Seriously?" She let out a series of disgusted noises but climbed off me. The sound of her zipper stroked along my dick as if it had been her finger. "Panties too?"

I bit my lower lip to keep the truth from escaping. She didn't have to remove them, but I desperately wanted her to. "Yes."

She mumbled about the stupid rules then lowered her body across my lap again. I closed my eyes in an exquisite agony of need, sliding my hand along her upper thigh. When my fingers encountered the curve of her ass, I had to carefully breathe past my need to orgasm. Her breasts were likely just as… small, firm, and…sweet. There was no other word for it.

"That is *not* spanking."

Her voice was muffled, like she had her face buried in the couch. "I have to find your ass, love. I'm blindfolded."

"Well find it already, Mr. Slow Hand."

Oh I had found it. And my cock was about to burst.

She squirmed. "You're still *rubbing* Lucian." Another squirm and I hissed.

"Fuck, I'm sorry." Major lie. "But if you keep moving like that…" Letting the words trail off, I raised my hand and brought it down with a firm smack.

She screeched and I soothed her skin.

"Rubbing!"

"It's how I spank baby."

"Don't rub me, just spank!"

God, she was infuriating. I gave her another smack and my hand soothed it in reflex.

"Lucian! I am the damn Dom. I said quit rubbing my ass!"

I gritted my teeth with the torture of not being able to. "Yes sir."

"Tara! I told you to call me Tara! Oh my God, you suck at subbing. You're going to lose points for us. Please do as you're told!"

I spanked her. I had to do it quickly or else I'd lose my mind. She squealed and kicked her legs but she didn't move from where she was. I stopped at ten, ready to fucking die.

"You're done?"

"Fuck, yes."

She got off and slapped me on the shoulder. "You didn't have to do it so hard. And why are you acting like it was so much work? It's my ass on fire, not yours."

God. "Aftercare."

"What!? For a spanking? What kind of wussies are making these rules? I'm fine. There's not a big enough Band-Aid, I'm sure.

I made a blind grab for her arm and pulled her into my lap.

"What are you doing?" Her voice squeaked with used up patience.

"When you get a spanking, you have to have after care. The end."

"Those are some awfully bold words for a sub."

"Please, Tara. Just… let me. It's required."

"So stupid." She squirmed some more. "What then? What do I do?"

I got on my knees next to the couch. "Lay here. On your stomach."

I imagined her staring and debating, doubting whether she could trust me. Judging by the non-compliance happening, she had some serious concerns.

She sighed and grumbled more about big BDSM babies, but she laid down.

I placed one hand on her back and held her while finding her ass with the other.

"So you're going to rub it all better? Are you kidding?"

I lowered my mouth to the hot skin and kissed softly.

"Oh my God! You're kissing my ass? Okay this is crazy."

I didn't hear her. All I heard was my blood rushing in my ears as I licked over the hot flesh then blew softly. I wish I had been paying attention to when she'd finally shut up. There was suddenly only silence as I administered kisses over every inch. I kissed along the crack, and she clenched her cheeks tight when I dipped my tongue. I placed my cheek on hers and slid it slowly all over, loving the feel. I stroked the flesh with my fingers, paying attention to her response. God if she'd just let me pleasure her.

Chapter Six

Dear Jesus, I should stop him. But really, it felt so good. And harmless. And good. As much as I was liking it, his need to do it seemed greater. And for that, I couldn't protest. In all honesty, he was being super sweet. Even if he was just trying to get me in the bed, he was still being really nice. And there was the whole blow-my-mind cuteness. And his *body*. Always naked! Always aroused. That wasn't helping me at all.

Wasn't that the point? Loosen up? Maybe it was a good time for that drink. What was he doing back there? I arched my hips a little when his touch lessened. I jumped at the soft glide of his finger between my butt cheeks. Yes, that. He slid it lower then back up, making me lift again, not wanting him to stop. His lips were on me again, his breath coming in hot gasps. His finger continued to tease along the lower part of my butt where other things began. I wanted his touch there. Again, he moved in the opposite direction. A grunt escaped me as I tried to give him better access.

"Open for me Tara." His hot words raced over my skin as he continued to lick and kiss. I had to. I had to open. Just a little. "That's it," he whispered.

His touch returned and I gasped at the pressure against my folds. Dear God. That felt good. He worked his finger inside me and I cried out, lifting my butt more. His finger sank in deep and I gasped. "Lucian."

"Oh fuck." The pained word preceded his lips sucking hard at my butt while he moved his finger in and out, slow and deep, with a flick when he was buried. His other hand slid firmly up my spine and into my hair and my moans wouldn't be stopped. He moved his finger in and out and the wet sounds made everything hotter somehow.

I rolled my hips, needing something more and he bit my butt with a groan, clamping his fingers in my hair.

The crazy switch flipped in my mind and in a flash, five years of *jiu-jitsu* self-defense training kicked in and I was suddenly on the floor with him, the offending appendage in a painful lock. "Don't you fucking pull my hair, don't you *ever* fucking pull my hair!"

"Tara!"

I realized what was happening to me and released him. "I'm sorry. Shit!" I soothed his arm, feeling awful. "I have hair pulling issues. And reflex… issues."

He jerked the blindfold off and I covered my mouth at the look of concern in his pretty blues. Now that was new. I'd not seen that kind of look in a man's eyes before, not while looking at me. Pushed some emotional buttons, didn't it? Shut that off. Shut that off now.

I laughed, trying to sound casual. "Crazy lady, sorry. It won't happen again. Unless you pull my hair. I… I don't do hair pulling."

"I see that." His voice was soft and astonished. Maybe worried.

I covered my privates, heat burning my cheeks now. "Okay, so. What's next?"

He stared at me, the question still in his gaze. God he had gorgeous eyes. I always had a weakness for blue eyed men. And his seemed to come with an array of…

emotions, and effects on me. I pointed to my clothes. "I need... to dress."

If he hadn't been *after ass caring* this wouldn't have happened, really. What the man needed was to learn restraint. An idea popped in my head. "Turn so I can dress please." I flicked my finger for him to hurry.

He lowered his gaze to my bottom and I stretched my t-shirt to the floor, hiding. A sexy small grin filled his mouth as he reached for my clothes. He threw my pants then twirled my underwear. "I knew it."

I raised my brows, reaching for them. He brought the underwear near his face and kept his gaze on me.

"Don't."

He turned into them and closed his eyes.

"Lucian, give me the fucking underwear. That's an order."

His brows filled with agony before he finally threw them at me.

"That's a good little slave. You know what you need?"

"Yes." It was a gasp of desperation. "I do."

"You need discipline, that's what you need." I got up and headed to the table near the couch. I picked up the list and sat, going through it. "Ah, foot worship. Now that I could do."

"You like feet?"

"No. You do. My feet." I scanned the list. "Oh, you're definitely going to turn me on with Forniphilia, later." At seeing his quirked brow, I smiled. "You'll be my bed."

"Fine, and when I'm Dom, I'll force you to wet in it."

I stared at him, the burn of his check-mate filling my face. God he'd better not.

"And by the way, everything you choose off of the list narrows down the selection for me. Thank you for that."

I chewed my lip and lowered my head.

"Don't Dom out on me now sweetheart."

I glared at him. "Screw you."

His eyes drifted shut with a slight shake of his head. "Yes. Please."

"Oh? You want to be screwed?" My hands trembled in anger as I scanned the list. "You want to be *pegged?* Mr. Bane? I can probably handle that."

His jaw worked slowly to the left, calculation in his heated gaze. "How many points is it?"

Shit.

He raised his gaze. "Well?"

"I'm not doing that."

"You're eventually going to have to get out of the kiddie section sweetheart if we're going to win this. I hope you know that. The Sadist in there probably has a thousand points. Now, do you need to win this fucking competition or not?"

I stared at the paper in my lap. "It's worth one hundred." I clenched my eyes shut. "Please, I can't. Not that. Something else." I sounded like a baby.

"What about..." I stared at the maybe options now. "Number...twelve."

"I don't have my book, love."

"Well... get it. I'm not going to *say* it."

"God forbid. Just so you *do* it."

"Yes, exactly. I don't need to sing about it."

He came back with his list and sat on the couch. He looked at me in astonishment after reading. "Really?"

I slapped my lap. "Seriously?"

"Okay. Now? Sorry, stupid question. Where?"

"Wherever, I don't care." I waved my hand.

"Right here."

The husky sound of his voice shot sparks through me. I really didn't mind doing things to him. That wasn't quite as bad as him doing it to me. I had control this way. "Get ready then." I picked up the blindfold. I wouldn't be able to watch.

"You already used the blindfold."

"Well I just won't get points for it then." He stood and I quickly tied it on tight. "Tell me when you're ready."

"I'm ready."

Dear God he sounded ready. His voice strained with anticipation. I felt my way to the couch until I encountered his hand. He guided me between his legs and I held on to his knees. Just oral. Like… like… puffing on a giant cigarette.

But I didn't smoke.

"Take your time sweetheart but, if you don't mind," he whispered, "please hurry the fuck up."

The strain in his voice said he was dying with need. And the idea that he needed it, actually made me not mind giving it. Odd. I slowly slid my hands over his legs, feeling my way. The intimacy of that made me wish I could see so I could go straight to the job site.

"I'm so fucking hard for you."

The nearly gasped words shot heat between my legs. I focused on the feel of him. His legs were warm and muscular. I wanted to really feel them but…

He took my hands and placed them on his cock and I let out a stupid yelp. "Okay. Okay."

"Yes." The desire in that word as he held my hands on him and pumped his hips… made me nearly dizzy. He continued moving the extremely large phallus between my hands. "Please suck me."

Oh dear God. I lowered until my lips found him, ready to forget everything. I opened my mouth and took the head between my lips.

"Oh my fucking God." He thrust slowly with a long hiss. Those sounds. Heat speared through my body as I held the length of him in both hands and began moving my lips over the thick top. "So perfect."

Encouraged, and yes, horny out of my mind now, I took more of him in, his taste growing on me until I sucked more, deeper, faster.

"Oh God, Tara!"

The devastation in his voice shook me. To think I had that power to give him this pleasure...I liked it. I liked to hear him feel good. I pulled up and licked all over the top and his hands gripped my head tight.

I gasped in fear that he'd pull my hair and I'd have a reflex again.

"Suck it, Tara... fucking don't stop, take it deep. Take it all for me."

I moaned desperately on him, doing it, wanting to give him anything he wanted. Everything. I skimmed my hands up his muscled abs, feeling him. Oh God, he was so beautiful, his body. I was suddenly hungry for all of it.

"Fuck! I'm coming baby." He grabbed my head and held it tight and bucked his hips. I cried out around his cock, my nails digging into his sides as I held on. "Can I fucking do it in your mouth!"

I could only nod frantically and he roared just as hot liquid hit the back of my throat. I knew that was the most foolish thing I could ever do, taking his semen into my *mouth*. The semen of a man who'd been with countless women. And yet… this one was mine. This one time. And I had to have it, this part of him. This very intimate part of him.

Chapter Seven

She was amazing. Fucking amazing. Sucked my cock like a champ then got right back to business like she'd done that kind of thing every day. Only I know she didn't. Docked the points, had me worship her feet and do some other bullshit item on her little to do list. But what pissed me off the most was how she wouldn't look at me. And why exactly did that piss me off?

I realized something as I laid naked and tied wide open on the play bed in the toy room. Her dominant nature was playing against mine. Keeping me from her. Well I knew how to fucking fix that.

"How long are you going to study it?" I watched her chew on her thumb nail while pacing nude before me, desperately searching the list in her hands. She was down to the nitty-gritty on her maybe list and had exhausted all the fluff. Pleasure or pain now.

She stopped pacing and looked at me. "Do you *have* to constantly *stare* at me?"

I let out a huge laugh. "Yes. Yes I fucking do."

"I thought you didn't do porn."

"Porn? Is that what you think you are? A Playboy centerfold?"

She faced me, only having her glare to point with. Her hands were busy, one covering her gorgeous pussy and her paper covering her breasts. "I know I'm not all that, you don't need to rub it in."

Dear God, this stupid woman. "You misunderstand love."

"Do I?"

"Yes you do."

"Don't try to lie and say I'm pretty."

"Not pretty. You're much more than that love. You're a super nova hitting my world and I can't turn away. I'm riveted in awe, wondering what the fuck is this angel doing in my dungeon?"

"Flattery. How cute."

"Just please fucking pick something, for Christ sake, my wrists and ankles are going numb and there's no points for that. So, if you're going to choose something sadistic, make it count."

She went back to pacing and I allowed my gaze to devour every inch of her delectable preoccupied body. She was about to get what she clearly needed for the past ten years. "Just know, when it's my turn... I'm choosing forced orgasm for you, love."

She stopped pacing and turned to me, her spine erect. But where oh where was the challenge in her eyes?

Dominance hummed through my body and brought a joyous curve to my lips. "I'm going to imprison you in pleasure. Until you're crying. Until you're begging. Until your well kept secrets are on fire and dripping down your thighs. I'm going to crush your sexy resistance with my lips and tongue. And I'm going to be right at your scorching mouth, eating up the sounds of your mind blowing orgasm until you say it-- no, until you scream it. Lucian. Lucian Bane. That's what I want you to scream while I milk the ecstasy from your pretty little soul."

She stood there in shock. I was wondering if she'd ever recover when she finally began to nod. "That's it. Play dirty."

"We're likely so far behind in the points, it's over. Do you really think they're not done with their entire lists?

Or at least all the big point items that we've not touched. It's not *if* they'll do the list, love, it's how well they do it. And in that regard, we are so losing our asses." But I'd known we would all along.

She pointed at me, revealing her breasts. "I don't need this from you. We're supposed to be a team. I can't do some of this stuff." She actually appeared hurt, like she knew it was going to be her fault they lost. But I was tired of playing.

"You should have thought about that before you signed up. And why can't you do the pleasure list, Tara. It's fucking pleasure, you won't die."

"It's not *just* pleasure. It's… I can't…" she opened her arms completely forgetting her nudity. "I can't just do those things with just anybody."

My cock stood tall and she went back to covering herself at seeing it, eyes all suspicious. "Well, when does one become more than just anybody to you, Tara? You have a formula for the human emotions?"

She stared at me and finally turned, presenting her backside.

"Oh God, baby, let me worship your ass. Choose Ass worship, I beg you. Or Face Sitting. I'll pay you." I pulled on the restraints in agitation. "Face Sitting is worth a lot. We need the points. It's just pleasure, love, and I'm tied up. You've masturbated before I'm sure? You can close your eyes and pretend that's all you're doing."

She paced and shook both her hands. "Okay. Okay, okay. I'll do it. But I have to bathe."

"Fuuuuuuck," I groaned.

"I'm not letting you do that unless I bathe. Ew."

"Can you fucking hurry?"

"Fine, fine."

I watched her go into the bathroom and closed my eyes, sheer joy racing through me. An eternal fucking hour later the shower shut off.

"Close your eyes. Please."

The timid way she demanded set me on fucking fire. What was it with her and that yin-yang behavior? Why did I like it so much?

"You must be a prune."

I felt her hand pressing on the small bed. "I'm climbing on you."

92

I was speechless as I waited. I suddenly wondered if I could have an orgasm this way. It'd be a first. Might even qualify for one of the bonus awards for most creative. Too bad they didn't have bonus points for most comical. We'd have that shit in the bag.

"Oh God, don't look," she whispered.

"Yes, Tara." It was a reminder to her that she was in control. It was also a reminder that this was a role we'd be switching.

"I'm. Ready."

Was she waiting for me to open my mouth? Stick out my tongue? I just never knew with her. Then I smelled her. Dear God. I leaned up instinctively and encountered smooth skin. "Oh Jesus, you shaved."

She squealed and moved out of reach. I laid my head down, somehow managing to keep my eyes closed. "I'm not chasing you. Plant your beautiful pussy on my mouth before I fucking scream."

"Okay, okay." The scared whisper throbbed right in my dick.

"Tara, your safe love. I promise I wouldn't ever hurt you. Tell me you believe that."

She answered by putting those sweet soft secrets right on my mouth. She kept enough distance that allowed me to make out with the full folds in a tender reverence.

I groaned on her. "Yes, just like that." I tilted my head, feeling her at different angles, then licked and sucked each petal between my lips. I slipped my tongue between the folds and slid it softly up. The ache in my cock drew a painful groan from me. I teased around her clit with the tip of my tongue and she soon began to sing those delicate worried moans. My hunger went to new dimensions with the sounds she made and I rode that current with her, kept her gripped with it.

I finally got her to the threshold where she could let go of her fears and embrace the desire. "Lucian, yes."

I could only gasp right on her, wishing she'd take over. "Make yourself feel good."

She gave the sweetest whimper and grabbed hold of my hair. Dear God. That. I moaned in sincere gratitude as she began moving herself on my mouth. Her hips rocked slowly at first then her fingers raked my scalp in tune to her delicate little pumps. And God, those precious whimpers and mewls were breaking me down.

Her moans picked up in speed and pitch, now. Her fingers no longer scraped, they pulled my hair, and holy fuck, she twirled and bucked herself on my mouth.

"Oh God! Lucian. Lucian."

I growled and sucked her clit into my mouth while she came apart on me, shudders racking her sweet body as her legs clamped my head.

I listened to her spiraling down from ecstasy, the angelic sound touching forbidden places inside me. I wasn't a religious man, but fuck, I was pretty sure I'd just heard the voice of God.

****

I took my time in the shower, letting the hot water pound some of the tension from my muscles. As a coping mechanism, it was fairly effective and quite harmless compared to many. And if I ever needed a way to decrease some of the shit going through my head, now was the time.

Just after Tara came apart on my mouth, a buzzer had sounded, followed by a recorded voice informing us we had one hour to prepare for dinner. The organizers were requiring all the contestants to participate in a semi-formal dinner each evening. The gatherings would serve several purposes, including announcements of the current scores and opportunities to accumulate bonus points.

The whole idea of meeting the other competitors over dinner made me nervous as hell. I'd be perfectly happy to go through the whole thing without knowing who our opponents were. That particular bit of information wouldn't change how I played the game. I just wanted to spend the time with Tara.

On the other side of the glass shower doors, she fussed with her hair and makeup, even though she was already perfect.

Finally, I could put it off no longer. I shut the water off and stepped out to dry off. Tara's gaze followed my reflection in the mirror. Satisfaction surged through my cock and I went up behind her. Standing so close the tip brushed against her ass cheek, I waited like a good sub.

A slight tip of her head invited my mouth to her neck and shoulder. I nibbled along the delicate column and she gave little moans in response. She leaned back a bit, bringing her shoulders to my chest, sighing as my arms went around her. God, I could hardly believe she was letting me.

The damn buzzer chose that moment to sound. "All contestants, please be prepared to exit your rooms in ten minutes. Once in the corridor, proceed to your left until you reach the dining room. Repeat…" The digital voice went over the instructions once more.

"Oh, we have to hurry." Tara darted away and into the bedroom.

I took my time dressing so I could watch her shimmy into a silky blue dress. She stepped into her sexy black heels while I buttoned my shirt. Five minutes later we stepped into the corridor and followed the directions toward the dining room.

Just ahead of us, I recognized Jase Duff's bulk moving through the double doors that must lead to our destination. A petite feminine form moved carefully at his side. Apparently he'd found a partner in the contest who fit his preferred victim profile. Guys like him had no shortage of willing prey.

I had to work hard to keep my disgust from showing as more than a scowl. The last thing I needed was to invite Duff's attention to Tara, or to lose points because I couldn't hold my temper. I kept Tara close and escorted her to the long table in a room of gold and crystal opulence, where the other contestants were in the process of finding their seats.

When everyone was seated, a team of white-jacketed waiters flooded into the room. Some delivered plates while others poured wine, and just as suddenly as they'd appeared, they were gone. Ten adults, including Tara and myself, sat at the big oval table, staring speculatively at one another.

"I might as well start." A big black man with a bald head and a huge grin stood. "I'm Reginald. The rest of you might as well go home." His large mouth opened and deep laughter boomed out like canon shots as he raised his glass, then lowered himself back down.

Duff stood. "I'm sure you all know who I am. This contest is simply a formality, a cash cow for the company. I've already won."

The others simply introduced themselves, without all the bravado and pissing contests. When my turn came, I just stated my name. I wasn't giving that bunch of half-baked assholes the respect of lifting a glass to them, much less *standing*. Tara followed my example, thankfully, rather than drawing attention to herself. The less reason Duff had for looking at her, the better, in my opinion.

As if my thought triggered his memory, Duff narrowed his eyes and looked at me closely. "Lucian Bane?" An ugly grin spread across his face. "I remember you and I owe you. Two of my best subs left because of you and I had to find a new play room."

"That wasn't because of me. It was because you're a mad dog that should have been put down long ago. Your subs left because they were tired of cleaning up your messes."

A tall skinny guy who'd introduced himself as Burt Mathers let out a guffaw. "This is the guy that got you kicked out of Mistress Stacia's? He looks like a vanilla puppy!"

Just what I needed. Another sadist to stir Duff up.

"Don't look so nervous, sweetie!" The middle-aged woman called Catherine, spoke from the other side of Tara. "The big bad Doms won't hurt your little boyfriend. Too bad." Her giggle sounded more like a deep rattle of phlegm. "But take some advice. If you want to play, you'll have to dress the part. You look like you took the wrong detour and ended up here instead of the PTA meeting."

Next to me, Tara stiffened. Don't bite the bait baby. Why didn't I tell her how these people would search for buttons to push? Glancing around the table, I chose impromptu weapons I could effectively defend her with if the need came.

"Well, Catherine, I'll take that as a compliment." Tara's voice carried enough to silence the other conversations.

Catherine grinned, nasty anticipation making her cruel green eyes glow. "Honey, I'm sorry, but it wasn't meant as a compliment." She rattled more phlegm in a forced laugh and glanced around the table, searching for approval from the others.

"Are you sure?" Tara's voice was pure silk. "As the PTA leader, let me educate you. My ability to blend in, to look normal, is what makes me, and guys like Lucian, the better Dom. See, we can have our kink, without having to look like circus freaks. We dominate both lifestyles, and no one has a clue."

A chuckle forced itself past my lips at the priceless words, despite the seriousness of the situation. How had I doubted she could handle herself?

Silence fell around the table, then laughter broke out. Apparently at least some of the others liked seeing Catherine fall on her face, including Duff whose laughter gunned out like a plastic machine gun.

Catherine scowled and glared at Tara. "Don't think this is over, little whore. When you least expect it, I'll be there to kick your ass."

Tara grinned. "Baby girl, when you feel like trying, come on. Bigger and badder than you have tried and failed. Of course, you wouldn't want to be disqualified here, would you?"

"Catherine, I think she's got you there." Duff tossed back the rest of his wine. "Bane, I think I've figured it out. She's the Dom. You're just here as her sub."

I kept my breathing under careful control and merely raised my glass in salute, agreeing like a good little peacemaker that I was. All the trash talk was yet another aspect of the lifestyle I didn't care for.

"Hello, everyone." The tall blonde who'd acted as announcer during the auditions approached the table. "I see you're all becoming acquainted."

A couple of the others greeted her, but she didn't bother to give her name to anyone. So, she considered herself The Domme in the room. Interesting.

"I'm sure you're all ready for updates?"

The table erupted in murmurs that amounted to affirmatives.

"First, assuming you're interested, I have some of the details for how you are being judged." She signaled someone out of sight behind her and the lights went down partway and a screen on the opposite wall lit up to display Gladiator, Inc.'s corporate logo. "You were aware coming in, that your suites were wired and that the footage would be available online via pay-per-view subscription. You haven't been privy to the scoring criteria, and you won't be until the end of the competition. Raw and natural talent. That is what we're looking for. We don't want play Doms, we want real Doms. And that is how we will find them. If you have it, you have it. If you don't…" She twirled her hand in the air with a roll of her eyes then turned back to the screen with a handheld remote.

"At the moment, Team Five is in last place." She quickly went through the scores and placings, in reverse. "And in first place, Mr. Burt and Catherine."

Tara and I'd made third. What a miracle. We were doing something right, maybe the creativity part.

Silence fell as everyone stared at the screen, each no doubt assessing their chances to gain enough points to win.

The blonde turned to go, but paused. "I would suggest you all try to get a good night's rest. Tomorrow is the group event and auction. You'll know details when you arrive." She took a half dozen steps. "Oh, and remember," she raised her finger in the air, "you're being judged *at all times*." Heels clicked on the tile floor as she left the room.

Chapter Eight

I sat next to Tara, holding her hand. Because that would hopefully ensure more respect if they thought we were an actual item. I hoped. I didn't know any of these people except the one I wished I didn't, so it was anyone's guess if it'd do a damn bit of good or not.

The dining room from last night had been cleared except for chairs grouped at one end. The tiled floor had been covered with utility carpet, and large covered crates sat against one wall. The blonde announcer stood before the group, all seated in the chairs. "The numbers you each wear represents your team. After you mingle for thirty minutes, we'll begin the group play. Basically, you'll each be required to perform, for the group, whatever you find in the envelope with your team's number on it. From the beginning, we deliberately withheld the standards we're using to judge you by, except for the general information you were given at dinner last night. We can't allow anyone to play to the judges."

Somewhere to my left, a female cleared her throat as if to speak, but the announcer didn't stop for her.

"And remember, the natural Dom is being judged. That means we don't want it to be merely a role you play when it's convenient, but who you truly are. A true Dom. The game begins on announcement via the PA system. Good luck."

Tara tugged me with her to the waiting envelopes on an elegantly engraved silver tray that rested atop a small, heavily carved table that stood in the exact center of the room, directly under the magnificent crystal chandelier.

She led the way to a secluded corner while I discreetly watched our opponents' faces, searching for some hint that might give us a competitive edge. Standing so that my body shielded her from the others, she opened the envelope. "Shit, flogging? Fifty lashes?"

My heart lurched as I peeked over her shoulder at the dreaded word on the page. "You'll flog me."

"What? No, I can't."

"You can't? No, I can't."

She grabbed my arm and pulled me closer and began hissing. "What do you mean you *can't?* You're a *Dom!*"

"So what?" I hissed back. "Did you think all Doms have to like making women hurt?"

Forehead scrunched up, she appeared to think about it. "Kind of."

"Maybe some do. Maybe even a lot. But that's not me."

"You cut me pretty good." Her voice betrayed her disbelief.

"Because *I had* to."

"You didn't seem to be too bothered."

"*Dead* wrong again." I shook my head. "You didn't notice I did everything I could to reduce the pain? To keep the cuts small and shallow? To keep your mind occupied?"

She glared at me, then rolled her eyes. "I don't want to beat you with a flogger! I'm not violent."

I raised my brows.

"Unless somebody pulls my hair." She looked over my shoulder, then back to my eyes. "Can't you pretend? One more time? It's only fifty lashes."

"Only *fifty*?" I wiped my hand over my mouth and shook my head.

"You spanked me. How's that different?"

"That was with my hand. And I can soothe you when I spank you." My mouth had gone dry with the desperation of my need to convince her.

"I'll let you soothe me after, I promise, you can… do whatever you want."

I raked my hand through my hair wanting to pull. Not being able to soothe her flesh with my tongue and lips after every lash would unravel my fucking mind and soul. Fifty times over. "You need to do it."

"I can't!" Her hiss had become a faint squeal and I worried she would draw unwanted attention.

"Why not? Just give me one good reason."

She stared at me, biting her lower lip. "I… I just don't want to hurt you."

Oh God. I turned away from the look in her eyes. Her words made it more impossible. I stood there fuming. Fuming with needs I didn't get. She moved to stand right in front of me.

"Just do it fast. I can take it. I promise. It's just pain. I have a very high tolerance as a woman, women do. We…have giant humans out of our vaginas. Think of the money."

I couldn't speak. I'd say something really weird and stupid that made no sense. "Fine. But if I do this…" She looked at me, tenderness in her gaze. "I…"

"Anything you want. It's yours."

"I know it is."

She quirked her brow. "I'm trying to be nice here, you don't need to be a dick."

"I'm just being honest."

"You're being cocky," she murmured, then looked around. "Interesting crowd."

I caught Duff looking my way and turned my back toward him, hiding Tara again. Sicko. "Remember what I said about that dude. Don't look at him. Don't look near him."

"I feel sorry for that girl with him." She leaned, trying to see.

I yanked her around. "I just said don't look!"

She grimaced. "Sorry." Her face remained pained as she held my gaze. She reached and patted my arm several times, the movements jerky. "You uh. Gonna be okay? We're number four, so, at least you won't have to wait so long to soothe me."

I could only glare at her while wanting to kiss her. "I know what I want for this."

She got serious. "Okay. What?"

"I want to know what happened to you that made you not like sex."

She looked around then swiveled her eyes back to mine with raised happy brows. "Okay."

"And no more not looking in my eyes after I suck your pussy."

"Oh geeze." She turned away a little, her cheeks going red.

"I need… to hold you a second."

She faced me, concern back in her eyes. "Okay. Like… a hug?"

I stepped up to her and put my arms around her. She embraced me back and I pulled her closer, rubbing along her back and butt, feeling her.

"Ooookay, public."

I tilted her chin up to me and stared into her eyes. "Can I kiss you?"

Her brows furrowed. "You're asking?"

I thought about that, realizing how odd it was. "I need to kiss you, but…" I closed my eyes, trying to figure out what the fuck was going on with me. "I don't want to *take* anything right now."

She held my gaze, seeming to hear me, understand me. She reached up and pulled my face to her lips and pecked them. I put my hand behind her head and really kissed her. God, the softness of her mouth… I'd been aching to feel it again. I wanted to do so much more with her, if only she'd allow me.

She pushed out of my arms and patted my chest. "That's quite enough public display of affection."

Is that what she thought I was doing it for?

A female voice came over the speaker. "Take your seats. The games begin in one minute."

The chairs had been replaced with small wicker loveseats with upholstered cushions. We made our way to the one marked number four. Tara leaned her head toward me. "Sounds like your girlfriend."

I wished I could enjoy her little remark, but every muscle in my body was in knots. Not just over the flogging, but the stupid auction. God help me if Tara were chosen to be auctioned. Of course, she wanted one of us to be picked. I prayed it would be me or neither of us. I didn't even want to think about Duff in that equation.

A large staged bedroom had been set up against the wall across from where we all sat, and was no doubt stocked with everything needed for the event. The first couple went up and a bondage assignment became apparent. I put my arm around Tara and pulled her closer.

"What are they doing?" Tara asked.

I took her hand in mine, aware of the dark sneer from Duff. "Looks like bondage."

The woman sat on the bed as the man worked quickly, looping a thin, dark rope about her body, knotting and looping more. As he worked, she began to look deformed, the rigging pulling tightly into her skin.

Tara made a small choked sound. "What the hell? Why?"

"They like it?"

"Why?"

I shrugged. "For the one being tied, it can be many things. She wants to demonstrate trust. She wants to feel controlled. She likes the excitement of danger that comes with being vulnerable. I'm sure there are many more reasons."

"And the… tier?"

"He can like the exact control. He can like the power. He can like knowing she's scared. He can like knowing he's trusted. He can like being creative with it." I nodded to the stage. "He clearly likes the artistic aspects."

"I'll say. She looks like a frick'n human waffle."

"And many like the marks it leaves after the rigging is removed. You don't want to meet a third degree Sadist who likes the artistic flare of bondage."

"Third degree sadist. A man who likes to hurt unwilling victims but not kill them."

I nodded.

She watched the demonstration a few seconds more. "Ew, right."

The little show lasted half an hour while the man bound her arms and torso. At the announcer's prompt that his allotted time was up, the man nodded and helped the woman off the stage to a seat at the side. There, he proceeded to remove the binding, taking care to rub circulation back into the skin as he went.

Team two made their way to the stage. The woman was flung against the bed where she began to struggle. At the first scream, Tara's nails bit into my palm, jolting me with shock. She hid her face in my arm and put her finger in her ear.

"Shhh, what's wrong?"

She shook her head and made humming noises like she was trying not to hear. I glanced around and caught that monster bastard with a huge grin on his face.

I pulled her closer and made soft noises to her. "They're only pretending, it's not real. It's not real."

God she was fucking trembling. Was this the reason for her frigidity? A past assault? Fuck. And I'd been so fucking insensitive and forward.

The tormenting act ended in a screaming orgasm. By then, the rest of the contestants were grinning and giggling at the little Dom lamb nearly in my lap. I wanted this fucking thing to be over so she could go back to her small town and forget this ever happened. And get her through this event without getting auctioned. She wouldn't quit, I was pretty sure. And I couldn't stand it if she got picked by that monster. Never.

"It's over?" She popped up and looked around. At the expressions on everyone's faces, she looked at me, regret filling her brow. "Shit, I'm sorry. I had a bad experience and I don't..." She shook her hands the way she sometimes did when extremely agitated. "I'm fine, I got therapy and-and everything, but sometimes it hits me, you know?" She nodded at me, her eyes full of worry.

I grabbed her face and kissed her lips repeatedly. "I get it. Stop. I get it. Don't fucking apologize for that. You're beautiful."

She took several calming breaths like it was a familiar routine she'd practiced. "I'm fine. I'm good."

The idea that she dealt with that alone for however long made me ache inside. Made me sick. Made me want to walk out of there with her, out of this life, this world and run away with her. Take care of her. Keep her safe.

The last bit would be a tad difficult with my past hunting me. I'd likely just get her killed, that's what I'd get.

I fucking needed to win this. But already we were so far from first place.

The second couple went into the little triage aftercare area and the third couple went up. If I wasn't careful, I'd vomit. We were next.

Tara hid her face on my shoulder. "Tell me what they're doing. I have triggers."

I placed my hand on her head, helping shield her as I watched the couple preparing. "It's… it's not bad. They're…acting out AB/DL."

She sucked in her breath and looked at the stage. "Adult baby…"

"Diaper love."

"Ohhhh my God."

The man got on the bed in his giant cloth diaper and began his act as a newborn infant, wailing and flailing his lanky limbs.

Tara burst out in snickers on my arm. "Why couldn't we get that?"

I looked at her with concern. "You want to play like a baby and piss and shit in diapers?"

She buried her face in my shoulder and stifled hysterical laughter. I had to smile and chuckle. Mostly at the amazing sound. I could definitely get used to hearing that.

"Oh look, she's nursing him."

Tara squealed as quietly as she could, kicking her feet and pulling my shirt.

I lowered my head. "Shhhh, it's not nice to laugh sweetheart."

"I'm sorry, I'm sorry, you're right."

I bit my lip at the laughter in her tone. The woman rocked the large baby for a few minutes.

"Cawwee me. Cawwee me." The man held his arms up to the woman and she lifted him.

He wrapped his lanky limbs around her and I snuck glances around to see if anybody else was as entertained, and found all watching in rapt attention.

I looked back at the dynamic duo on stage just in time to see the woman lose her footing.

"Oh shit." Tara and I both leaned forward as the couple fell off the stage into a heap of limbs.

Loud booming laughter erupted from the couple on the floor and Tara followed suit. I watched her, speechless as she howled. God, she was so… not of my lifestyle.

Genuine. Authentic. Sweet as fuck, even when she was trying to be mean. I'd wager she didn't have one deceptive bone in her body, that everything about her was decent.

The couple left the stage and Tara looked at me. My heart dropped. Our turn.

Chapter Nine

I made my way with her to the stage and pointed at the flogging horse.

"I lay on it?"

"I tie you to it. You have to be nude, love." The regret and shame in my tone drew her gaze.

She came and kissed me on the cheek. "I'm sorry Lucian," she whispered. "I think it's the sweetest thing that you hate hurting me. But I need you to do this, please. Do it quick and I'll make it up to you."

"Don't." I shook my head, unable to look at her. "Don't offer anything for this. Nothing is worth it."

"Okay." She hurried and removed her clothes and I restrained her. I picked up the flogger and raised it. Then lowered it when the strength left my arm.

"Awkward, Lucian," she whispered.

I hardened my jaw and resolve. "Get ready. I'm doing it quick so hold the fuck on."

I made it to fifteen and stopped. I paced a few feet, wanting to kill.

"Just hurry. Finish."

The sound of her strained breaths tore my heart out. "Fuck!" I began again, aiming in different spots. She jerked left and right, her yelps killing me. *Don't stop, don't stop. Don't you fucking stop. You're a fucking Dom. You dominate shit. Now dominate this and get it over*. At forty-five, I couldn't see through my tears. I hurried to finish, feeling so fucking dirty.

On fifty, I threw the flogger down and hurried to her. "Fuck baby, I'm sorry."

She jerked to me. "Lucian! Lucian!"

I couldn't make myself look at her.

"Look at me. Look at me!" Her words were harsh and lassoed my sanity.

I finally looked at her,

"I'm okay, see? Didn't even cry. Now untie me so you can hold me."

I hurried and did as she said and pulled her into my lap when she was free. I stroked her body softly and carefully, rocking her, kissing her everywhere I could reach. I didn't care who saw. Fuck them. Fuck all of them sick bastards.

****

God, I'd never seen Lucian so upset. What had happened to him to make him hate hurting a woman? I wasn't the only one with issues, that's for sure. I let him comfort me until he was satisfied. The manager came on the stage to tell him to take me to the aftercare area. He promptly replied with, "Fuck you."

I waved the man off. "Lucian, sweetie, I'm fine. I'd like to get my clothes on. Okay?"

He looked at me. "Yeah. Yes, get dressed. I'll help you."

We went back to the couch and Lucian seemed miserable. I put my arm around him, trying not to wince and make him feel horrible. He laid his head on my shoulder. "God I wish this was over already."

I stroked his hair, my heart tugging hard in my chest. "Soon. Hold on for me?" I ruffled his hair a little.

He sat up and looked at me. "I have issues too, love."

"Pff." I tossed my hand. "Who doesn't?"

"Oh God, what a fucking monster," Lucian mumbled, eyes on the stage now.

I looked out and my stomach tensed at seeing that ugly giant of a man making that poor girl get on her hands and knees. "What…"

"Pony play." The disgust in Lucian's voice was lethal. "The one being the pony isn't usually made to carry weight they can't possibly sustain. Unless it's at the discretion of an idiot like him."

I grabbed his hand. "Do I need to turn away?" The guy put a leather apparatus on the poor girl's head, forcing something into her mouth as he did.

"I may need to. Of course he'd sit his fat fucking ass on her." Lucian's voice carried and he didn't seem to care. Was glad.

"Okay, shhh."

Lucian made a disgusted sound and turned his head away when the guy began talking trash to her. He slapped her in the head, making her hair fly. "Fuck." Lucian sat back.

I grabbed his hand and squeezed. He was still upset over the flogging. This was bad. I could feel the tension in his body needing unleashing.

The man jerked on the leather reins leading to the girl's mouth, then slapped her butt, hard. "Take your master for a ride, you stupid cunt!" He let out a laugh like a fat demon while the girl walked him around the stage on her hands and knees. Her arms and legs trembled visibly from the strain of carrying him.

"Oh God." I looked around to see if any of them would do something. "Her... her mouth is bleeding."

Lucian leaned forward and lowered his head, shaking it.

The man delivered rapid blows to the girl's rear with a meaty open palm while she slowly crawled with him. "Hurry, you slow bitch. Giddy up!" Another evil laugh followed. "You better not make me late! I'm goin' to DOM WARS!" He roared the words then whacked at her rear. The blows sounded more like punches than slaps.

She suddenly collapsed under his weight. "What the *fuck?*" He got up and dragged her up by the reins. "What's the matter, jackass? Don't tell me you're tired." He slapped her across the face and she landed on her side.

Lucian shot up. "Come the *fuck on!* That's enough!"

I stood and held his arm while the guy turned wide eyes to him. "What's the matter?" He yanked the girl up by her hair and shook her like a rag doll. "You don't like to see pretty little girls hurting?" He twisted his fat face into mock sadness.

"Lisa. You can tell him to stop," Lucian called. "They'll make him stop. Just say the word, sweetheart."

"You know she don't want to stop." This came from the female in team three on the right. She grinned showing a few missing teeth. "She likes it."

Lucian spun to her. "How do you fucking know? How do you fucking know?" he roared.

The lady's bean pole of a man stood up. "Now calm down."

"She's fucking broken!" Lucian pointed at the girl. "How broken does she have to be? How pathetic does she have to be? She just wants acceptance and love. She lets him break her because she wants to make somebody fucking happy!" Lucian looked at the psycho. "You can't make a fucking devil happy!"

Several Dungeon Managers had gathered around Lucian, seeming ready to escort him out. "Get it together or you're out." A big black guy next to him spoke with a cautious hand stretched out.

Lucian put his hands up. "I'm fine. I'm fucking fine."

"This is your first and final warning. Another outburst will cost your team."

I pulled Lucian back to the chair, our corner, feeling like we were in a cage fight with a bunch of animals.

"We'll take a thirty minute break and then have the auction." The Dungeon Manager who'd spoken to Lucian scanned the room. "Afterward, you can return to your rooms. You'll have until midnight to work your points. Winners will be announced tomorrow at the formal munch."

God, we were almost done. Now if only I could get auctioned. Or Lucian. That would be a thousand points. We could win it then. Lucian pulled me into the corner next to a large artificial tree. I looked at him and my heart raced at the angst in his eyes. He lowered his lips to mine and kissed me with a hunger that speared my tummy, his hand firmly on my jaw, his other hand cradling the back of my head.

He broke the kiss but kept his lips next to mine. "Let's just quit. You want to?"

My heart lurched. "Lucian."

He pulled up and held my face. "Fuck this, it's not worth it. You're too good for all of this. Please."

"We've come this far, Lucian. I can't. I have to finish, I'm not quitting."

His eyes rolled shut and he put his forehead on mine. "If… you get auctioned. I'm quitting."

"No. No, you can't do that. If you quit, I lose, you can't do that to me." I shook my hands, panic rising.

"Why does it fucking matter?"

"Because my Gramma is…"

He looked up with closed eyes. "Fuck, I knew it. I knew the moment I helped you pick up change from that adorable tin can that you were a fucking saint." He lowered his head and shook it. "What do you need, love? Maybe I can help you and you won't need to do this."

"A lot of money. To bring her home," I whispered, mostly because my throat was closing. "She…she's in a nursing home, she had a stroke. She needs special care. I can't leave her there, I need to bring her home."

He covered his mouth then held her shoulders. "She's old love, that's what we sometimes have to do—"

"No." I shook my head as panic set in. "She's not that old. She's my Gramma and she raised me when my mother and father abandoned me, she's like my mom, my friend, you have to help me. She-she's crying and begging me, please Lucian." I dug my nails into his arms my final words barely audible squeaks.

He pulled me into a tight hug and gasped in my ear. "Okay love. Shhhh. I told you I would help you. I'll help you."

I pushed out of his arms to see his face. "You won't quit?"

He sighed and lowered his head. "I won't quit." He met my gaze and stroked my cheek with his thumb. "I knew you were different sweetheart."

I nodded. "I knew you were too."

He gave me that sexy smile. "Did you?"

I nodded wiping tears. "I did."

"Time's up. Back to your seats for the auction."

Chapter Ten

We returned to the loveseat and Lucian made me sit in his lap this time. I felt awkward being held like a baby and at the same time it felt… so very amazing.

The lady that had led us to our room strode out with an envelope, her voluptuous body on display in a skin tight red leather body suit and thigh high spiked leather boots. Red. Miss Red.

My leg jumped up and down and I chewed my thumb nail while Lucian sat like stone.

The woman's lips curved like a snake as she opened the envelope and pulled out a card. Her eyebrows raised. "Tara from team four is to be auctioned—"

"Mother fuck." Lucian slumped a little like he'd been holding his breath.

"And the contestant who gets his bonus time with our lovely Tara is…"

Lucian was back to rigid and I held my breath.

"Burt Mathers from team three."

Again Lucian slumped in relief, I hoped, before bringing his mouth to my ear. "If he selects anything sexual, or physically painful, you're done."

"I can handle it Lucian." I made my whisper harsh so he wouldn't know how nervous I was. "I'll quit if I can't." He sat back and I turned his face to me. "I'll quit myself if I can't handle it. I know what I can handle. You have to trust me on this one. Lots of years of therapy, okay? Degree in psychology."

He stared at me, his eyes calculating. "Remember what I said."

His hard voice and the brutal look in his eyes were entirely new to me, and sent a shiver up my spine. I nodded and he went back to brooding.

"Will the contestants come up please?"

****

The second Tara left the couch, a surge of energy bolted through me, leaving every muscle locked with a new domination whose middle name was Rage. I could barely breathe as the crushing power held me in a vice, burning like demonic acid in my bones. I stood *behind* the couch needing a barrier for the moment, something to prevent me from throttling someone.

If that man did *one thing* to Tara, he would die. Locked and loaded, I eyed the man called Burt as he strolled like Mr. Normal and stood to the right of the woman in red. I suddenly realized *not* knowing the man might be more dangerous. The only thing I'd gotten from supper about him was that he knew Duff. That in itself didn't speak well for the man.

They walked to the stage and I followed, stopping at the very edge of the allowed perimeter, leaving maybe twenty feet between myself and him. I'd need the momentum of speed if I had to step in. My heart thundered in my chest and I struggled to bring it under control.

The man leaned his head toward Tara and talked in her ear. I couldn't see her face and I walked along the perimeter for a better angle, straining to hear the low mumbling. She nodded rapidly, mumbled something and I tensed as he nodded as well. They'd agreed to something.

The man finally stepped away and circled her until he stood at her shoulder. He remained there for nearly a minute, looking down at her like a predator sniffing his meal. What the fuck did he have planned? She'd made a lot of button-pressing remarks at supper the night before, but I couldn't be sure if any of his had been selected. Maybe all. And I didn't know what monster lurked behind the door leading to that dungeon in his soul.

Tara stood with her eyes closed. The fact that I could see her chest moving from where I stood said she was scared. What was he fucking doing? God I wished he'd do it. Just…do it. Put your fucking hands on her. I silently willed him to cross a line, any line. I took mental note of where bodies were that might try to stop me, calculating several scenarios.

I froze as he slid a hand up Tara's arm furthest from me. His hand made it to her shoulder, and she slowly raised it in a cringe. Was he just going to intimidate her? I could handle that.

He finally made his move. The wrong move. His hand wrapped in her hair and he jerked her head back. It was like lighting an extremely short fuse and Tara exploded like dynamite, slamming the man on the floor much the way she'd done with me, sending my adrenalin into overdrive and the audience behind me to their feet.

"You can't. Fucking pull. My hair. I *just* told you that."

The man grunted in pain with his face smashed to the floor, arm pulled up and back in a painful hold.

Tara looked at me and gave me an *I got it baby* nod, while panting.

"I'm sorry," the man gasped.

"You're sorry?" Tara gave a light chuckle and pulled his arm harder, making him scream. "Ohhh, now *that* sounds a little more like sorry."

A new energy mixed with my fear as I watched her. Hope. Pride.

"I'm sorry, I'm sorry." The man's voice broke like a boy in puberty.

"You gonna let a *girl* take you?" Duff sneered from somewhere behind me. "I'd fucking kill that bitch."

I gritted my teeth, resisting the temptation to unleash my pent up rage on that Berlin wall behind me.

"I'm going to let you up." Tara adjusted her grip. "And you can try again, okay?"

"Okay." Little spineless prick.

Tara let him go, and he grabbed and flipped her. Before I could react, Tara escaped and grappling ensued as he tried to get an advantage.

It nearly killed me, not stepping in, but she was handling it. I went back to the invisible track I paced on the floor, and watched.

The guy gained a second of leverage and whooped in celebration. Then Tara flipped him hard and wrapped herself in his legs. The guy screamed and banged his hand on the floor.

"Woohoo," Tara yelled then laughed. "Didn't see that coming, huh?"

He thrashed in agony as she put more pressure on his knee. Fuck, was she going to break it? That would cost her. Oh God, I'd pay her. I couldn't pay her enough to snap it, just snap his fucking knee baby and let's walk the fuck out of here.

What a fucking thrill. I got to watch her nearly break both legs and even his back before the timer went up. When it did, the Dungeon Managers came in to ensure everything was okay. They took the man to triage and Tara hurried to me.

Duff came out of fucking nowhere to her right. "I got your party, bitch."

I didn't make it in time. I didn't fucking make it. He slammed his head into hers and she dropped limp to the floor.

My heart stopped and before it started back, I was running and Duff's face was getting closer.

Rage screamed like a tornado in my ears. Then I was airborne, train-wrecking into Duff, praying I could take him apart before they stopped me.

Knowing I wouldn't get a second chance, I aimed for his face, fingers like ready daggers. My right thumb found treasure and I dug in.

His scream erupted as I was yanked off of him. But I'd got him. He thrashed beneath the men tending him, holding his eye. At the sight of blood on his hand, I smiled, so fucking happy. So. Fucking. Happy.

"She's coming around."

I jerked to see Tara sitting up and fought to go to her. "Let me go. Let me go to her, fucking let me go!"

She struggled to get to her feet, reaching a hand to me. The look on her face fucking broke me. She was sorry. She was sorry.

And I was fucking in love. I was so. Fucking. In love with her.

Chapter Eleven

I sat on the couch back in our room, my body once again coiled and tight. But now it was with other things. Needs. Too many. Too strange. It was my turn to Dom and I was beside myself with how exactly I would do that. I had Tara cooking for me. Still clothed. I was terrified to scare her. Terrified with the need to take her in a way that might get my ass handed to me. Terrified that I might actually want that. Need it.

She'd touched something in me that day I got pinned by her. That thing in me. That odd hunger that sent me running out of the BDSM community and into a soul search. Beneath the initial shock of her strength, it was there, that reckless energy deep inside, wanting something, something to do with her, something to do with…something. I needed to figure out what.

I mean, was I not a true Dom? Was she actually more of a Dom than I was? What the fuck *was* a Dom anyway? Who wrote these definitions into the manual?

Who decided who I was? No fucking body. I did. I decided.

Now I had a more pressing and immediate decision to make. We didn't know what would come of the little circus we'd just left. We didn't even know if she earned the bonus points and if she did, whether or not I'd lost them for her. I didn't know what she was thinking because she wouldn't fucking look me in the eyes since we got back to the room. So, my guess was, nothing good.

How was I supposed to play Dom for points while she was upset with me? I didn't want to *play* Dom with her and I especially didn't want to do it for points.

My tongue moved restlessly in my mouth, watching her in the kitchen, fantasizing. Not about how many ways I wanted to fuck her, or taste her, but about having her entirely. While I fucked her and tasted her.

And what was it with me and eyes lately? Since when did it bother me for a woman not to look me in the eyes? Never. But with her, I needed her to. I needed to see what I did to her, what I caused in her. I wanted to be on her mouth, in her mind, I wanted to bind her the way she bound me with just one kiss.

God no. It was one look. I saw it when our gazes first locked, picking up change on the ground. It was right there, this... fucking heaven. And it sank its beautiful nails into my heart until I ached for the mystery of it. The something amazing. The something I needed to get lost in. Get found in.

"Tara."

"Uh, yes?"

"Can we talk?"

"Sure."

Her light answer told me she was in that mode. Hell, she was always in it. Problem was, I needed to get around it. She sat across from me, letting me know we were back to somewhat friends. A pressure gathered in my chest and I took a deep breath around it. "You said you'd tell me."

"Oh. Yeah." She angled her gaze up and clasped her hands in her lap, posture erect. "Well..." Her tone was light, like she were about to take a walk down memory lane in a casual omniscient voice. "When I was nineteen. I was gang raped in college."

She actually met my gaze with a little smile and nod and I thought I'd be sick. I stared at her then finally lowered my gaze, unable to take the look in her eyes. I shook my head a little trying to understand why I couldn't stand it.

"How do you do it?"

"Do what?"

"Pretend."

She narrowed her gaze a bit. "Pretend what?"

"That you're not in a prison."

She gave a little laugh and stared at me, almost guarded. "I don't pretend." She shook her head a little, looking offended. "Why would you say that? I know who I am. I know what I feel. I know I have issues, I deal with them the best I can." She dusted off something from her legs as if to demonstrate. "I have OCD because of the trauma, PTSD, I have an endless list of phobias that I've inherited from the event."

"I'm sorry."

"For what?"

"I should have been more sensitive."

"Pfft. How would you know?"

"There are plenty of signs."

"Ohhh, I imagine there are. But to assume they lead to that would take a mind reader."

I stared at her, that pressure in my chest nearly hurting. "You're so fucking beautiful, you know that? No, don't. Don't look away. Look at me. Please."

She kept her eyes down, her brows furrowed.

"You can't pretend with me. I guess I'm glad, I hate pretenders. But I can't tell you how much it kills me to think your mind sees me as a threat."

She nodded, still not meeting my gaze then finally pointed at me. "Ah yes. You hate to hurt women. I have to wonder what happened to you to set you so vehemently against that."

"You think it's unnatural to not want to hurt women?"

She looked at me finally, her professional mask on. I suddenly wanted to crush it into a million pieces so she couldn't hide from me. "Of course it's not unnatural. But I think you display an unnatural amount of anguish over it. Have you noticed?"

It was my turn to look away. Yes I knew, I noticed. If anybody else had, they'd never said it. "I think it was from having to paddle my little sister once."

She didn't say anything and I took a deep breath. If I told her, would she open up to me? It was worth a shot. "I was twelve and...my little sister was told not to play by the creek by the house. I was told to watch her. She was only four. Well, being an average twelve year old, I got distracted, and Rachel did as she was told not to do..." I shrugged, fingering the hem on my pants. "My father came home and discovered it and she was punished. And I was made to paddle her." I slowly scraped my teeth over my lower lip. "I'd never been so... fucking hurt by something. It wasn't her fault, it was mine. I should have been the one punished and I begged for him to punish me not her, told him he could give me as many paddles as he liked. No, he'd said. This is the better punishment. This way you will never forget again. And he was right. I never forgot." I couldn't look up at her, the weight of that shame burning through me fresh.

"What... did she think?"

Pain speared my chest and I gasped. "She cried and begged me to stop. I was too scared of my father doing it instead though, so I did it. He made me give her ten spankings with the paddle. She was only four." I grit my teeth as tears burned in my eyes "She… she wanted to comfort me after," I whispered. "She was such… a sweetheart. I'd cried more than she did and she wanted to comfort me." I shook my head in eternal fucking regret. "And the fucking bastard wouldn't let her."

"I'm so sorry."

I nodded. "Me too. I've never told anybody that. Too fucking ashamed."

"I understand."

I wiped my face and looked at her. "You understand shame? For something you didn't really deserve?"

She nodded. "Yes. I do. I feel it from what happened, there's nothing really I can do about it." She shrugged a little and smiled.

"That," I said.

"That?"

"That pretense. That it doesn't hurt."

"Hurt? Not so much. Angry, yes."

142

She was in denial. That's what it was. And until she dealt with the pain, she'd never get past it. It was the same for me, but I never had a reason to deal with it. Her pain needed dealing with because it kept her from living. It kept her from feeling. And it kept her from me.

"I'm the Dom tonight."

Her walls shot up and pain hit me. It didn't matter how much that hurt. It didn't matter that it was like having my baby sister afraid of me. I had promises to keep. I had chains to break. And I had a woman to free.

And pleasure was my rod of iron.

"You remember what I promised to do to you love?"

She clasped her hands together and cleared her throat a little. "Yep. I do." She scraped at her fingernails. "I do."

"Say it for me."

"I'd rather not."

"I'm the Dom tonight, love. That means you do as I say. And call me master. Unless of course you're ready to quit."

She shook her head while looking off to the right. "No. No quitting. Just... tell me what to do. Master."

I didn't know what ached more. My heart or my cock. "I want you to say it. Tell me what I'm going to do to you."

"Forced orgasm." She tossed the word out.

"Yes. Forced orgasm. I'm going to tie you up. And I'm going to worship every inch of your body. With my lips. My tongue. My fingers. And my cock. Now, stand up. And undress for me. Slowly."

My detailed description had shaken her. Not as much as it had me. To say the words out loud got me so hard.

"Right now?"

"Right now."

She hesitated briefly. "Can I pay you extra to get out of this?"

"You forget I'm willing to *pay* to be able to do it." And that was still true.

"Fine." There was that anger she'd encased her pain in. The one I needed to crush. She stood and began to undress.

"Slower."

She huffed and slowed down and I watched her ass come into view only to clench my eyes shut at seeing red welts. God damn.

"Turn to me." I waited a few seconds and opened my eyes. She stood completely nude hands covering herself.

I looked at her. "Can you guess what I'm going to tell you next?"

She took a deep breath and looked up with only her eyeballs then dropped her arms.

"Very good. So very good. Now come here." I stood and waited for her to obey, my eyes locked on her breasts. The need to adore them took the strength from my legs. She stopped before me, her gaze on my chest. "Undress me now."

She rolled her eyes slowly up to meet mine with a *really* look. She shook her head a little and began shoving my shirt up over my abs. I leaned a little so she could pull it over my head.

"Get on your knees. And take off my pants."

She dropped to her knees and did as I said, her movements still jerky and pissed. That was okay. For now.

When all of my clothes were off I whispered, "Touch me."

"Where?"

"Everywhere."

"Starting from?"

"My feet. With your lips."

She gave a snort and mumbled as she lowered to the floor and began kissing my feet with hard loud smacks, working her way up my legs. It was difficult not to smile but I really needed to make this count.

"You missed a spot." I pushed her back down to her knees, my hand on her head. "I hope you know I'm being a very kind master right now. And while your ass may be too sore for spanking, your pretty pussy isn't."

I held my cock and waved it at her. "Here, love."

"I know where it is, Jesus, it's not like I can miss it."

"That was my thought. And yet you did."

"I didn't *miss* it."

"So you disobeyed?"

"I guess you can call it that."

"Now I have to punish you."

"More than you are?"

Fuck. Too bad I wasn't into masochism because her words and cold tone would be giving me a fucking orgasm. I let more of my Dom surface. "Lay on the couch Tara. On your back."

Like a two year old, she got up and stomped to the couch and laid down like a person in a coffin.

I went over and stood next to her. "Look at me."

She looked at me.

"Open your legs wide for me."

She shut her eyes and opened her legs about half of what I needed.

"Wider love. And look at me."

She opened them a little more and I could see I'd have to tell her ten more times before I got them as wide as I wanted. I took her right leg and put it on the top of the couch. I took her left leg and pushed it down, then moved her knee toward her shoulder.

"I want you open. Very open. Now put your hands above your heads. Like they're bound. If you can't figure it out, I'll bind you literally."

She closed her eyes again and did it.

"Look at me."

She finally managed to pry her eyes open, the pain and anger in the depths saying we still had a long way to go.

I braced my hand on her ankle, pressing it into the couch as I slid my fingers over her inner thighs. "I'm going to lick you here." I stroked along her open folds, letting my finger dip barely. "Your body tells on you, love. You're so wet. And hot." I barely touched her clit and she gave me my first point. A tiny moan. The first vocalized of very many to come.

"Am I right? Is it hot right here?" Again I whispered my finger over her clit a few times.

She strained against the pleasure and nodded.

"I know love." I teased barely at her entrance. "I'm going to finger you until you're bucking on my hand like a good girl."

She was there. On fire. Ready to listen.

I used my entire hand to softly caress her sex, feeling the exact shape of her. I delivered a sharp smack to the puckered lips and she yelped in surprise. I rubbed it softly, tickling at her clit then sliding down for a tease at her dripping entrance. "Your pussy says you like that." I dipped the tip of my finger in her opening, wetting it. I licked it, and shuddered at how good she tasted. Smelled. "You're fucking delicious baby."

She whimpered and I answered with another firm smack. She arched her back and squirmed, keeping her arms obediently above her head. "I told you I would make you squirm, love. Did you not believe me?" I plunged my finger inside her and she cried out. "Mmm. You're so fucking wet. You hear it?" I jabbed deep and quick then switched to slow sensual, then again to shallow fast. "You're so tight on my finger."

I pulled out, gliding my finger softly over silk to adore her clit with lazy circles, then flicks, making her writhe, moan, and buck her hips. I knelt next to her, needing to taste. The hard tips of her nipples demanded my attention, driving my desire to that reckless point. I smacked her pussy and tended to her breasts with dominance, filling my mouth with as much of the firm mound as I could. I sucked then let it slowly glide out to hold it captive between my lips for vigorous flicks of my tongue.

She broke the invisible bond I'd put on her wrists and buried her fingers in my hair. Joy surged through me and I moved to her mouth to lick and kiss. "This is for breaking your bonds, love." I spanked her pussy and consumed the sweet cry she gave in my mouth. "This is for taking so fucking long to break it." I plunged my finger deep inside her.

"Lucian."

"Yes. Say it." I rammed my finger against that secret doorway, intent on breaking through. "Say it baby."

All of her control flailed like leaves in an errant wind. "Lucian. Lucian."

"Fuck, baby. I can hear it. I hear all your beautiful secrets in my name. I want them. I want you. All of you. Give me what's fucking mine."

I placed the palm of my hand against her clit putting circular pressure while I continued to unlock paradise from inside. I tasted the passion pouring out of her in rippling, unstoppable waves. Hearing her orgasm approach, I lifted my head to watch it, watch as she let it all go for me.

"Lucian! Yes, oh God!"

I watched as my hand and fingers stripped away her control and burst through that prison entrapping her. I kissed her. "Break for me. Come undone baby, I'm here. I'm here, you're safe."

She suddenly pulled me against her, nails raking my skin, and that sweet body arched hard into mine as her orgasm trembled through her with a desperate cry of freedom. In my ear. In my heart. Fucking amazing.

But I was hardly done.

Chapter Twelve

I waited in the aftermath for a verdict, my head on her chest, listening to her heart. It was hammering out the truth and I waited. Waited for what usually crept back in. The walls.

"Okay. That was. That had to be."

I held my breath.

"Had to be a lot of um... points."

I raised my head and stared at her. If her words hadn't shot my hope to hell, that averted gaze did.

Round two.

I pulled my finger out of her slowly and she made tiny noises. I put it in my mouth and sucked her off of me before standing.

Time for some bondage.

"Go shower love. Five minutes. Then meet me in the play room. Do not make me come get you."

I walked to the toy room and waited next to the wall of various bondage sets. How did I want her? In each position. She arrived on time and I held my hand out to her. "Did you like it?"

"Like what?" She looked around and took my hand.

"How I made you feel."

She gave that snort. "It was an orgasm. What's not to like about it? Geeze."

"Because you have those all the time, I'm sure."

"No, but if I did, they'd feel just like that."

"This is what we're doing. I'm going to tie you to this wall here. Your arms will be bound up here." I pointed to the location. "And your knees will be bound here."

She made a painful sound. "Are you sure that's physically possible? I'm not a contortionist."

I moved her to the wall and tied her hands first. "Are you ready for another orgasm?"

"I… can't honestly say if that's possible. Never had more than one in a day. Or…week."

I'd change that if I had my way. I lifted her onto my waist and held her against the wall with my body while securing her knees in the holds. "I'll be able to lick your ass like this. I've been meaning to do that ever since we met."

"Ew! God nooo! No!"

"Oh God yes."

"Lucian, that's... you can get diseases from that."

"You just bathed, love."

I pulled back and she panicked. "No don't, don't. Stay. Stay right there."

I quirked my brow and pressed my abs into her body. "Why?"

She swallowed.

"Think quickly, sweetheart."

"Because...I don't want to hang from here. I feel stupid."

I slowly lowered my eyes over her body until I stared at where her sex pressed into me. "Nothing stupid about you. Like this. With me."

"I'm not with you, I'm hanging on a wall."

I leaned in and nibbled at her lips. "What are you saying, love. You'll have to spell it out."

"Take me down?"

"I'm going to. But you haven't screamed my name yet."

"I'm... I'm not a screamer."

I lowered to my knees despite her protests. I stared at her pretty pussy eye level with me now. I stroked my fingers along her thighs then softly over her beautiful spread folds.

"Please…"

"Please. That's a good start." I looked up the line of her body. "I'll make a deal with you."

Her head jerked down and I chose that moment to kiss her clit.

"I'll untie you if you ride me."

"Ride you? Like a pony ride?"

I slowly shook my head no with my lips buried in her folds, sliding my tongue over her clit as I did.

"Ride you? Intercourse?"

I closed my eyes, suddenly not liking the term. She might as well have said porn. Any other word would've worked probably. I lowered my mouth, distracted with the feel of her silk on my tongue and lips. I licked as far inside her entrance as I could, my nose pressing into her clit. Reminded me of when she'd sat on my face. Fucking amazing.

"Is this… is this what you do to all your… your sex slaves?"

The foul words stopped me and I pulled away and looked up at her. "Sex slaves?"

"Subs, whatever." Her voice was shallow, like she was well on her way to losing herself again. But…

"I don't have any subs, love."

This drew her surprised gaze. "No subs? A Dom with no subs?"

"Not anymore." The idea that she was jealous suddenly had my cock raging with need. "Do you want me to?"

She gave that snort. I was figuring out she did that when she was about to lie. "As if I care."

My heart raced. "I can go get one to play with us. Would you like that?"

"Ummm,no. Not into threesomes."

I stood now, wanting to see her up close. "What are you into?"

"Nothing. Really. But if I were, it wouldn't be this, I can assure you."

"This as in…"

"Me, you. Here."

Pain stabbed me. "Me. You. Here."

"Can you take me down? My legs are hurting."

"No. I can't. Why not me, you, here?"

She gasped an incredulous laugh. "You're a Dom. I'm a... normal human."

"Funny, you told me you were a Dom too."

"Not the way you are."

"Oh, you mean the way I make you feel good?"

"Yes, that and... the whole lifestyle. I'm like..."

"Frigid?"

She stared at me, her jaw going hard. "I'm not frigid. I just don't like to be tied to a wall like a fucking two legged spider."

"Okay, then what do you like to do? Tell me. I'll do that."

She pursed her lips at me. "Fine, untie me and I'll show you."

"By all means." I quickly helped her down, knowing good and well she didn't have a goddamn thing she liked to do.

I waited while she stretched her limbs back to normal and, then she ran. I stood there, in shock, watching her slam the bathroom door. That was the last thing I'd expected of her.

I walked to the door and knocked with my knuckle. "What the fuck are you doing?"

"Being a brat."

I shook my head with a dry laugh. "I don't recall agreeing to that."

"Well... you're the Dom. Isn't it your job to Dom your subs? You clearly failed."

"You might want to step away from the door."

"What?"

I slammed my shoulder into the light door and it opened with a splintering crack along the jamb. "I clearly have failed to Dom properly."

She eyed me with escape in her wild gaze.

"Don't even try it love."

"I'll hurt you," she warned.

"You'll hurt me? You do seem to be good at that. Go ahead sweetheart. Try."

She froze for a few seconds then made a dash right at me. I let her pass then lunged for her the second she did. We both fell to the floor and I fought for control. Fuck she was strong. She grunted as she repeatedly tried to grab various parts of my body. I didn't know *jiu jitsu*, but I had pretty good fighting instincts and common sense.

I roared when she got my arm in one of those holds. "Bad Dom, baby."

"Ffffffuck." I banged my other hand on the floor in pain, trying to move into the hold. I finally broke out and again we grappled like tight rubber-bands. I finally managed a top mount. She smiled with her legs wrapped around me and I realized I'd only thought I'd managed something. Even though I was on top, she clearly had an advantage. I couldn't move. But did I fucking want to? My cock throbbed painfully. Her strength was such a turn on, especially when it rubbed exactly up against mine. I wanted to fuck her so bad in that second. Just like that.

Winded, I gazed into her eyes. "Why don't you trust me?" I hadn't meant for the question to sound so fucking desperate and broken.

She froze and stared at me. "Why should I?"

"I just..." I dropped my head to her chest, not wanting to fight against her. "I just want..." What did I fucking want? "I want you."

She let out a sound that said she misunderstood me.

I lifted my head. "Not sex, Tara. You."

She stared at me again. She was looking at me. Seeing. "Why? Why would you? You can get any girl you want. Why would you want me?"

God, her words confused me. "Why would I want anybody else? Don't you see who you are? How beautiful? You think I'm doing all of this for pleasure?"

"Money?" The word was tiny and full of pain, like she'd thought that's what it was all along.

"I didn't lie to you when I said I'd pay to help you win. I would have. Because you were so fucking sweet. And then when I got to know you, I didn't care about the game, I just wanted to be with you." I stroked her cheek with a finger. "But you're trapped inside yourself. And all I want is for you to be free and happy."

She turned her tear filled gaze to the side and pain speared me.

"Why do you always shut me out?"

"I don't shut you out," she gasped.

"Every time I set you free, you run further from me. What the fuck am I doing wrong? Tell me so I can fix it. So you see that I fucking love you."

She gasped and pulled me down and kissed me. Fuck. Yes. I just needed to beg? I kissed her back, my hunger erupting like a volcano inside. "I need you."

"Oh God, I'm sorry," she cried in my mouth. "I didn't know." Her hands raked over my body, trails of flame reaching to my bones. "I was scared of you because I…"

I broke the kiss and looked at her, needing to know why she was scared.

Her face crimped and she let out a sob. "Because you made me feel again. Because I thought I'd never be able to. Because I never wanted to. You scared me so bad because of how much I wanted you and every time you looked at me, touched me, spoke to me, you took something from me that I knew I'd never get back. I was losing myself in you and I was scared."

I dove on her mouth, devouring those words, her breath that held them, her cries that fueled them.

"I fucking love you." I pressed my face against hers, my heart bursting with emotion.

"Make love to me," she whispered, her fingers digging into my ass.

I shuddered hard at those words, those impossible words. Love. Blindsided by love. That's what this beautiful fucking mess was in me.

"I should get..."

She shook her head, regret and sorrow grooved in her forehead, her mouth trembling. "I can't get pregnant."

Her fragile whisper undid me until I couldn't breathe from the fucking pain in my chest. I dropped my forehead to her shoulder. "I'm so sorry, love."

She suddenly clutched me tight to her and let out a huge sob that led to another.

I held her in a fierce embrace and rocked her. "Let it out love. I'm so sorry. I'm here. I'll help you."

The pain making its way out of her was fucking monstrous, her body was rigid with it while her vocal chords tore with the intensity. She screamed and wailed out the agony as I kept her locked in my arms, murmuring every syllable I could imagine right in her ear, willing it into her mind, her heart.

Eventually her cries slowed to pitiful low wails, a steady slow current of grief. But the fucking avalanche had passed. And she still held on to me.

She still held on to me.

Chapter Thirteen

"Can I bathe you?" I whispered the words with kisses along Tara's shoulder, working my way up her neck, loving the delicate whimpers she gave. I would move mountains just to hear those.

"Yes."

I clenched my eyes tight at that one word. I'd almost given up on ever hearing it. With that one little syllable, so inconsequential, she had just given me the entire world. She'd given me her trust, the keys to her heart and soul to do with as I pleased. And all I wanted was to love her.

I took her hand and led her into the glass enclosed shower then set the water nice and hot. I turned her into the stream and stood before her.

She remained with her head lowered. "The whole world saw."

I tilted her face up at hearing the tiny words.

"Saw you what, love?"

164

Shame filled her eyes before she lowered them to the right. "Saw me fall apart."

I took her face in my hands and kissed her lips as softly as I could, so amazed with her. "What they saw was a hero baby. That's what you are. A survivor. A strong woman. Beautiful... Funny as hell…. Sexy…. Sweet…."

I was prepared to go on and on at seeing the slight smile taking over her lips. But my breath caught when she grabbed hold of my cock with both hands. "I'm an excellent marksman, too."

I gasped as she swirled her fingers over the head of my cock. "I see that." My breath shuddered out and I braced my palms on the shower walls, dizzy.

"It's your turn baby. Let me set you free."

I opened my eyes as she lowered to her knees. I shook my head and pulled her up, pushing her against the shower wall. "I need my cock deep inside you. I have to fuck you so very hard and fast. I'll fucking die if I don't, and I'm ready to beg."

She answered with breathless whimpers, igniting that inner hunger. I lifted her on my waist and growled when Tara's new passion greeted mine. We clashed like lightning bolts of desire and I trembled as I hurried to get inside her, fingers biting with desperate need. Finally I sheathed my cock in her fiery silk.

The rapture from that initial thrust exacted a roar from me, a shocked scream from her. Fuck, this was it. The one. The difference. The Alpha and the Omega. I pulled Tara against my body, needing her closer as I slid her along my cock, my hips managing slow erotic rolls.

Tara cried out in my ear. "Lucian! Oh God!"

She was the fucking tabernacle, the holy of holies. I moved inside her, placed her back against the shower wall, and held her arms at her sides ready to crucify her with our first time. I watched myself moving in and out her, marking my own mind, feeling everything fall away as Tara gave herself to me. The emotional rush that accompanied the soul branding was unlike anything I'd ever experienced, and again, I recognized the ultimate peak for what it was. It was the ultimate. The peak.

And fuck how my angel sang for me. She fucking sang the song of my soul. She made it rain fire down my spine, tingling, hard, licking into my balls and cock. My hips moved to its urgent demand.

The fire was beyond me, made me its beast. I threw my head back with a roar, my thrusts matching our heartbeats. The glorious orgasm gripped me in its relentless clutch and I jerked Tara against me, wanting her tight in my arms for my first plunge into that one way abyss of *This.*

"Oh God. Oh God." Tara's was right behind me. Still in orbit, I grabbed her waist, needing to see her sweet body meeting mine. I watched her in rapture as she fucking came undone, arcing with the shatter of walls inside her. "Lucian!"

Oh fuck, she'd screamed it. I pressed her face to mine and Tara let out a sob in my ear and I gasped at the sound, what it meant. Free. My baby was free. Fuck, yes. Chills ran over my body as the last shudder of orgasm rippled through me. We'd made the jump. Together. Lost ourselves in each other. God, I loved her.

I panted in ecstasy's aftermath, my soul on fire from the binding. I couldn't see it, but I could feel it. That Formal Collar. That ultimate bondage. A tidal wave of holy fuck slammed me as I tasted what this ultimate collar really was. It wasn't the ultimate prison, as so many thought. Or the final game. It was the ultimate freedom. The ultimate game.

And we'd just christened the playing field.

****

Midafternoon. The buzzer sounded followed by an announcement directing the contestants to the dining room again. Tara and I had packed our belongings, ready to depart the mansion. No doubt we were disqualified, after I injured Duff. It didn't matter. I'd have done it all over again.

I paced near the door, waiting for Tara. Anticipation of seeing her in a formal gown had my hands shaking. What would she wear? Something opulent? Or simply elegant? My vote was for simple and elegant. Her natural beauty would overshadow anything else and make it look like a rag.

Some sense alerted me and I turned in time to catch her standing still, staring at me with an odd look in those hazel eyes. She stood there in a ruby red silk sheath that left her shoulders bare and clung to every curve.

I felt like I'd been punched in the gut, blindsided by her beauty. I stood there like a dumbstruck fool, just staring at her.

The buzzer woke me, calling us to the dining room. I offered her my hand and she moved forward to take it. Before we left the room, I paused and turned her to me. "I can't go out there without knowing."

"What?"

I slid my thumb along her cheek. "That no matter how this turns out... you're mine."

She swallowed with a small smile. "Maybe."

Excitement erupted in my stomach and groin at the sweet challenge in her warm gaze.

"If you let me." I lowered and kissed along her neck. "I have things planned."

Her breath hit my cheek as I worked along her jaw. "Tell me."

I shuddered. "I really liked the way you screamed my name."

A gasp escaped her and I stroked my fingers along the pulse in her neck.

"I need that from you, baby. Every day. Your pleasure. I have so many toys I want to use on you, so many roles to play. Will you let me?"

She answered with a whimpered yes that lit me on fire.

I made her look at me. "As far as I'm concerned, we both won. I'll help you find a way to get your grandmother home. Okay?"

She nodded and fanned her eyes when they teared up.

I kissed her forehead and held my arm out to her. She smiled with a blush and I led her to the dining room, hand in hand, lost in some kind of haze that isolated us from the rest of the world.

At the door of the dining room, a maître de in a black tux showed us to our seats. This time each couple had a small, intimate table. We took our seats and as soon as all the couples were in place, the waiters approached laden with plates.

The moment everyone was served, the wait-staff disappeared, leaving us to sit and wait for things to get underway. To my surprise, Duff came in wearing a pirate style eye-patch, led carefully by the woman he'd so abused the day before.

The blonde announcer came in as we ate, again dressed to the hilt in her executive mistress attire. The only thing that really hinted at her lifestyle, was the narrow straps of studded leather that laced Roman-style up her shapely calves. "We'd like to encourage you to mix and interact following your meal. But I'm sure you're very anxious to know who won, and why, so we'll get that part out of the way. We also have some further surprises for you."

She strolled around through the tables, her wireless microphone occasionally squealing with feedback. "First, we must thank Gladiator, Inc. for sponsoring this competition. Dom World dot com and Submit dot com joined together to provide this lavish setting for us." A murmur of surprise went through the contestants.

"And without further ado… the moment you've all been waiting for…" The screen behind her illuminated, displaying Gladiator, Inc.'s corporate logo again. She pressed a button on the control device in her hand and the screen changed. "Contestants were judged on various things. As you knew, every item on the assignments list came with point values, as did the various toys you could implement in those assignments. What you didn't know you were being judged for was your ability to dominate in every aspect of the lifestyle." She turned to the contestants. "Many people confuse a Dom personality with a Dom's position of authority. The two are not exactly the same or interchangeable. A true Dom dominates. Plain and simple. And by dominate, we mean does what it takes to get a job done. Even if that means submit."

She turned back to the screen. "The third thing you were judged on, is interaction. How well you worked with your partner in each role you chose. During the assignments, after, and between. All of this matters in the real world of BDSM. And that is the criteria by which we judged."

Again she turned to the screen and clicked her little button. "I'll announce the scores and then I'll announce the demerits. There were quite a few, sorry to say." She signaled to somebody in the room and the lights dimmed. "Team One accumulated a total of 354." Another click. "Team Two: 734." Click. "Team Three made 1,768." My

172

heart hammered my chest and I squeezed Tara's hand. "Team Four: 1,550."

I gasped in relief and Tara clapped happily. They'd given her the bonus.

"And Team Five: 421 points."

"We lost?" Tara whispered.

I shook my head with an *I'm not sure* look.

"The next announcement is the demerits. Starting with Team One: -75. Team two. -0. Team Three. -250." My heart slammed my chest and Tara's nails dug in my palm. "Team Four:" She searched us out with a look of regret. "-1,550. And finally, Team 5: -421 points.

"We lost all our points?" Tara shrilled in small voice.

I pulled her hand to my lips and kissed it. "I'm sorry, love."

"As I've said, we have a surprise." She turned off the monitor and faced us. "What you also didn't know about this competition, is that it's not over. This was a competition of elimination. And we've eliminated all but one team who will go on..." she paused for emphasis, "to represent our country in a GLOBAL DOM WARS."

173

She grinned and clapped and everybody followed suit. I put my arm around Tara who sat there, head down on the table.

"But before you get excited, I have one more announcement. As you know, this entire thing was broadcast live online. Well... we decided early on that we'd let our audience participate in the judging. And so they were given the ability to vote. We also decided that each vote would represent a point."

Tara's head popped up at hearing this.

"Team Three." She faced them. "You guys *dominated* the first two days. But something happened on day three that changed that. A particular couple did something that apparently the audience really liked. And they earned over a million points. In three hours."

She turned to us next. "Tara Reese and Lucian Bane. You dominated. Then you failed. And then you dominated the hearts of the viewers on day three. You will represent our country in the global DOM WARS."

Oh holy fuck. She ended with clapping and everybody slowly followed suit while Tara jumped on me, nearly knocking me out of the chair. "We won! We won! Oh my God, we won!"

I crushed her to me in a rush of relief and shock. "Yes, love. We fucking did."

When the noise settled down, the woman said, "The two of you will be up against nineteen other couples from all over the world that won the Dom Wars segment for their geographical region."

Jase Duff growled. "This was rigged from the start! Those two don't know anything about the lifestyle, don't have any connections. Hell, they could pass for store clerks!"

The announcer smiled and approached him. "You fail to understand Gladiator, Inc.'s goal with this competition. We want to bring the BDSM lifestyle into every soccer mom's bedroom around the world. By showing that someone can look completely normal and still have a fulfilling kink life, we're making it acceptable for the lady with the white picket fence and two point five kids to enjoy the flogger and being bound. Her husband will no longer be considered a deviant because he wants to have her trust and have control over their sexual pleasure."

The announcer continued. "You, sir, and others like you, will scare average people away from the lifestyle like rats off a sinking ship, and lure varmints to the scene of that crime."

She turned back to Tara and me. "The next phase starts in seventy-two hours. We'll fill you in on what you need to know before the competition starts. But I'll tell you this much. In the upcoming challenges, you'll be judged individually and as a team." She looked at Tara. "And let me just say, honey. You might really want to work on your submissiveness, because if your team's sub fails to perform as specified in the events, the Dom will be punished for his lack of effectiveness. Which includes having to auction his sub to the top ranking Dom based on daily scores for the temporary training from a more qualified Dom."

Oh fuck.

Tara's brows went higher with each bit of information. "But wait, why does Lucian have to be the Dom? I'm a Dom too, maybe even better than he is. Right, babe?"

My stomach was in knots with this news. Especially with knowing how fucking fantastic a sub Tara wasn't. "We might want to talk about this, Tara."

"Talk about what?"

"Who is more qualified."

"But I'm not good at subbing, can't you?"

"We'll talk about it later."

She rolled her eyes. "Fine. But if you think about it, you'll recall how well I did with Domming. I—"

"Tara!" I glared at her with raised brows. "Can we talk about it later?"

She stared at me, her mouth open, looking from me to the woman standing there with a huge knowing grin.

"Ohhh, she gonna get *sold!* Watch!" This from the phlegm woman followed by loud laughter. "Who wants to bet?" Chatter and laughter immediately erupted in the room in agreement.

"Fine. Fine, I'll be quiet. I'll talk later, we'll talk later. And make the right decision." Tara's mouth finally shut as she stared at me and I could only assume she'd gotten the message I'd been telepathically screaming at her.

"What?" she nearly mouthed.

Dear God was there ever a more perfect picture of un-submissiveness?

She flicked her finger between the two of us. "We need to talk about this."

All the joy and rapture I'd felt five minutes earlier when we were announced the winners, slowly fizzled away. We'd gone from the fun and rush of the Pony Express, to the fear and complexity of a runaway train full of horse shit.

How about a sneak peak of round two?

Chapter One

I sat across from Lucian in the small interrogation-style room, him in one chair, me in another, maybe five feet between us. Facing each other, both of us nude. My nerves had me shaking like we were in a refrigerator. And there he sat like a sexy god, hands relaxed on his upper thighs, posture upright and legs open.

I couldn't tell if he was trying to intimidate me, or if he was just that damn cocky. Probably both. Either was a wasted effort with the mortification of what I was about to do suffocating me.

No talking allowed until we began, so I waited in the nerve-wracking silence for the bell that would begin the first test. *Masturbation climax race*. Really? Could it get any more embarrassing? And pointless? No touching each other would be permitted and the first to orgasm would win the right to Dom in the mysterious test following immediately after. And we would gain individual points.

And the challenge in the next round would be determined by the winner of this test. Like, what, the Dom-matrix? Ridiculous. God only knew what we were being judged on, but I sure hoped it wasn't grace and style.

I was torn on strategy. Should I watch him masturbate or shut my eyes while I did my own thing? As embarrassing as it was to watch, it was also arousing as all get-out. God he was beautiful. The muscles in his thick legs were tight and standing out. And judging by his extremely erect cock, he was ready for orgasm at the sound of the bell. No fair. And yet the sight of him like that had me excited out of my mind, so there was that.

I needed to prime myself the way he clearly was. I forced my gaze between his legs. Even his pubic hair was sexy. Black, fine, and short. Like he trimmed it. The veins on his cock were thick and made my tongue restless and my stomach flip. The memory of him sliding in and out of my mouth and hitting the back of my throat brought a runaway whimper. I swallowed it down as I stared at that gorgeous hard on.

He'd been silky, the skin of his cock, and at the same time impossibly hard. *"You're fucking delicious."* The image of him sucking my essence off of his finger blasted heat through me. My womb tightened with the throbbing in my clit as I moved my gaze slowly up, letting his hairless torso and chest fan my flames. He was the delicious one. Dear. God. He didn't seem to be a sunbather but the effect was a decadent hunk with cream-covered muscles. Dessert.

At finding his thousand-degree blue gaze burning through me, my breath caught. He bit on his lower lip and agony crimped the skin between his dark brows. The need in his face sent my pulse pounding in my ears. Jesus, I needed air. I parted my lips and filled my lungs with it just as the bell sounded and scared the shit out of me.

"God, your nipples are fucking killing me." The words blasted out like he'd been waiting to say them while holding his breath.

My cheeks burned and I covered my eyes with one hand, and quickly began rubbing my clit with the other. Fuck I was so *rusty* at this! And the groan Lucian gave told me I'd just shoved him down the orgasm slide.

****

I opened my legs wide and riveted my gaze on Tara's plump folds now wiggling with her middle and ring fingers, pinky in the air like royalty having tea. I stroked my cock slowly, letting my eyes roam her body, letting the view of her playing with her pussy drive heat into my dick. She had that lower lip tight between her teeth and her lickable tits bounced with her efforts. Reminded me of all the positions I still needed to fuck her in. I held my balls, using my middle finger to stroke that spot just beyond, sending hard heat licking along my spine.

She opened her legs wider and gave a strained whimper. "Fuck yes," I whispered, "You should finger yourself, love." Because that shit would send me over the edge.

She gasped and left her lips parted. Opened her legs wider.

"Yes, fuck your finger, you're fucking making me crazy."

More strained sounds came from her, seemingly frustrated.

"My cock is on fucking fire baby, don't stop."

She jerked her hand away from her eyes. "Stop talking! You're messing me up!"

"Jesus Christ, love, maybe you should watch me." I opened wider for her. "Do you see what I'm doing? Put your fingers back on your clit."

She stared between my legs and began rubbing again.

"Yes, that does something for you, love? Seeing my hand on my hard cock?" The hiss she gave answered for her. I gave my approval in a hungry grunt, sliding my hand over the slick pulsating head of my cock. "I'm going to Dom you so fucking hard tonight baby. Fuck your sweet ass with my tongue. You want that?"

She drew a sharp breath, then ran her fingers over her nipple, bringing my orgasm within reach. Her tiny moans and grunts licked my balls and she finished me off by lifting her knees up with the slightest whisper. "Lucian."

"Oh, fuck yes." I threw my head back and let it come, let my long hard groans signal my victory as I came so fucking hard.

"Uuuugh! This is stupid!" Tara's growl whined with desire and frustration and I had to laugh. But I was so relieved. Giving up the Dom role in any challenge outside of sex wasn't something I was remotely good at. But then neither was she, clearly. And that could spell disaster.

"It's just a game." Desire still raced through my body and took the lighthearted note out of it.

I watched her adorable ass as she hurried to the corner and got her clothes. She'd folded hers and put them next to mine. For some reason it had bothered me. The folding, I got. It was part of that controlling nature she had. I understood that. It was her putting them deliberately and exactly six inches from mine. That's what bothered me. I was willing to wager she'd mentally measured out a distance. I didn't like it because it meant she still had walls up. And I'd deliberately not folded mine to show her I had more self-control. Only, she didn't see it as self-control, but lack thereof. But for me to not fold my clothes took more restraint than anything.

"Just a game, it's not just a game." She fought to get her feet in her panties, snagging her toe and nearly falling.

"Can you throw me my t-shirt?"

She grabbed at my pile without looking and slung clothes at me. I kept my gaze on her, silent remorse filling me with every body part she covered.

"God, you're beautiful."

"Yeah, everything's beautiful because you won." She yanked her t-shirt down and plopped to the floor with her legs drawn, arms crossed on her knees. "And what the hell does a climax race prove about dominance?"

I grinned at her while wiping my mess up. She was so fucking cute pouting. I'd win the next round, along with the right to dominate tonight. And then I'd spank her for all of it. My cock jumped at the thought of aftercare. "Maybe it proves I have more control?"

She narrowed those hazel eyes on me, full of *don't be a moron, moron.*

I couldn't stop my chuckle. "You're so fucking sexy when you're pissed."

That got me an eye roll and then that thing she did. Looking off to the right. That crushing feeling hit my chest at the reminder. All that progress I'd made with her was gone.

I got up and she quickly threw the rest of my clothes at me, like she didn't want me near her. And I wished it was over losing the game. But it wasn't. It was those same walls I tore down before. They were right the fuck back up.

I got dressed and held my hand down to her. She looked at it then up at me.

"We're a team, love. Even though we're also competing against each other, I need you to help me."

She rolled her eyes and put her hand in mine and let me pull her to her feet. The need to kiss her ran me over and I stole a soft one before wrapping her in my arms. I hugged her tight, resisting her need to push away and hide. "You okay, love?" I glided my mouth along her hair, knowing she wasn't.

"I'm fine."

The tension in her body was nearly debilitating. "Relax." I stroked along her back, working at the tension, pressing my face into hers, wanting nothing more than to kiss her until she forgot everything but what I made her feel. Alive. New. Whole. Didn't she want that? Need it? "I have you, love."

There was a slight give in her resistance and I took it with hunger, pulling her closer. It was enough. For now.

****

An envelope suddenly slid into the room from under the door and Tara shoved out of my arms to get it. She ripped it open and I couldn't deny the excitement of the challenge coming. And not knowing what it was gave me an extra thrill.

She mumbled frantically as she speed-read then half choked. "Are. You. Serious?" She jerked wide eyes to me, sending my heart on a stampede.

"What?" It was so fucking hard not to give in to the urge to run over and yank the paper from her, but we were being graded. Calm and collected. Control. The Dom power trait had to be exuded.

"I'm supposed to let *you* dangle me off a cliff? What is this bullshit?" She tossed the letter into the air and I caught it before it fell, the adrenalin rush tingling through me.

"We can do this, no problem."

"Oh yeah, sure, *you'd* say that. You're the one holding the rope. I'm the one risking my ass."

"We'll both be secured. Come on, it sounds fun. Unless you're scared of heights." I winced. "That would suck."

"No I'm not scared of heights." She was pacing now and biting her thumb nail.

"Are you sure?"

"This is soooo stupid." She shook both hands in what I'd come to recognize as one of her many ways of coping with anxiety.

I looked at the challenge. "At least we might get a helicopter ride to the top of the… whatever we'll be on."

She took deep breaths and let them out. "Oh yeah." She nodded, belying her frail-sounding tone. "If we get the answer right to the question, the one that demonstrates how well we know one another." She flicked her finger between us. "Should be easy. We've known each other for three whole days."

Wow. Three days. Seemed so much longer to me. "I think I know you pretty well."

"Bah!" She finally stopped and faced me, one hand on her hip. She gestured toward me. "Sure. Okay. And I know you too. Only no, I don't. See--" she raised her brows, "I'm a tad more practical than that. So what's my favorite food? Hm? Dessert? Flower? Color? Book, smell, movie, song? Animal? I don't even like animals, bet you'd never guess that."

"Well... if we get the question wrong, I just have to carry you."

"On your back! Up a mountain! Now that's total domination! Takes a real *Dom* for that. Only no, it doesn't. It takes a man with muscles and stupidity."

Seemed like kick-ass domination in my mind. "It's okay if you're scared."

"I'm not! I'm pissed!"

"For not being able to be Dom?"

"No!" She looked around as though searching for the culprit then huffed her disgust. "For having to masturbate in front of you for one, and..." She covered her face with both hands.

"I think you should have won that just for being so fucking hot, really."

"Shit."

"What?"

She pushed hair behind her ears and her hand trembled. I hurried over and she held up both hands as though to ward me off. "I'm okay. Yes, I'm... scared. Not like panic attack scared, but scared as in I don't want to go up there and do that scared."

I forced my way through her barricade and embraced her before she could run. "I get that. Totally get it." I stroked her back, up and down, my fingers having fun along her vertebra. "But...you will, though?"

I waited for her answer in the silence, then finally felt her head barely nod. "I will. For Gramma."

Chapter Two

The old pickup bouncing me and Lucian up the mountain had seen better days forty years ago. The lanky old driver cackled with laughter every time he nearly tossed us from the truck. The clutch groaned and I involuntarily braced myself, ready to bail the instant it showed signs of tumbling back down the trail. Couldn't chew my thumbnail because I needed both hands to hold on.

Watching the scenery crawl past didn't help, either. The so-called trail was really just a rutted out slash that zig-zagged through the heavy forest of the lower slope of the mountain. Every jolt across a stump or rock made me grateful for the sturdy cargo jeans and hiking boots I'd been given to wear. There'd been nothing in my bag remotely suitable for this expedition, that's for sure.

The truck suddenly tilted at a dangerous angle, throwing me hard against Lucian's side before I could brace myself. With an eerie crunching growl, the truck managed to right itself. Lucky me, I didn't get thrown into the driver's lap that time. I'd rather not have his bony knee jammed up my butt with his raucous laughter again, thank you.

The driver leaned his half bald head forward for the fifth time to speak around me to direct his words at Lucian, and I certainly didn't object. "You'll be five hundred feet up but don't worry," he yelled, like he was hard of hearing. "You'll be tied and there are safety nets." Burst of laughter. "So you won't *die*."

If we made it there alive. Jesus, I wished he would just drive, instead of constantly fiddling with the radio, or tapping a greasy hand on his stained jeans in time to whatever fragment of a song he managed to pick up. I braced one hand on the dashboard and dug my nails into Lucian's palm. He'd taken my hand a few minutes into the ride and I'd let him.

God, what was wrong with me? Why was I so nervous around him? Like the more intimate we were, the more I needed space. Cold feet? He wasn't proposing, he was just… being sweet. Then there was the whole sex stuff. I mean we *did* things. For this *game*. For *money*. It just seemed *weird,* a BDSM fly-by-night carnival. I wanted to trust him, but it was too much like falling for the cute carny working one of the rides!

We finally arrived to the destination, a broad grassy terrace carved into the side of the mountain. A black helicopter crouched at the edge of the flat area like a dragonfly ready to leap into space. A hundred yards away, a striped lawn canopy had been erected, and half a dozen people waited under its shelter.

Several minutes later, we approached the leggy Lucian-loving blonde, grinning from ear to diamond-studded ear. "Congratulations Lucian, on your victory earlier. That means you get to play the Dom role in this challenge. You will take control the way you're so good at doing, and Tara will submit to your direction the way she's…" eruption of glamorous laughter, ha ha ha haaa, so fucking funny. Dumb bitch. "And Tara will prove us all wrong and show us that she *can* submit to Sir Lucian Bane."

"My pleasure." I nodded and shook *Sir* Lucian's hand from mine to tighten my pony-tail.

"Well, as you know, you get a chance to hitch a ride to the top." Blinding smile. "All you guys have to do is answer one question correctly about each other. The first priority in the D/s life is to know your partner inside and out." She lifted one hand in a casual gesture and a diminutive man wearing a black business suit placed an envelope on her upturned palm. "Open it, open it," she muttered, handing it back, keeping her thousand-watt smile carefully in place while she waited. Glancing at the card, she aimed sparkling green eyes at Lucian. "Doms first."

My lids fluttered as I fought to keep my eyes from rolling.

"We asked Tara some questions on the application and one of them was, 'What part of a man's body do you like the most?'" She raised her brows at Lucian who now regarded me with contemplative brows. Great. I'd lied and said his butt, thinking it would gain me BDSM points.

"I'd have to say…she's definitely an ass girl."

My brows shot up in shock. "Oh my God, you got it!"

"Yes he did, now let's see if Tara knows you as well as you know her."

By her nauseating tone, she was so sure I didn't. I hated it, but she was likely right. "Is it the same question?" If it was, I was sure I knew the answer to that.

"Yes. Same question."

"Definitely her butt."

My heart sank at her stupid frown. "Awwww, no. He said all of her."

"What? That's not an answer." I looked at him. "What kind of answer is that? How am I supposed to guess that?"

"I didn't answer it thinking you'd have to guess, Tara."

I rolled my eyes. "So we lose? He has to carry me?"

"I'm afraid so, sweetie." With a sugary bullshit smile, she pointed to the rope ladder spanning a twenty-foot cliff we would have to get up before the trail to the top even started. "Hope you've eaten your Wheaties, Lucian. You have quite the burden to bear."

What was that supposed to mean? My gaze landed on her ample cleavage. Before I could say something about him not having to carry a milk cow around, Lucian grabbed my hand.

The way he squeezed my fingers said he knew exactly what I was about to say. He lifted my hand to his lips to drop a soft kiss on my knuckles. "She's light as a feather."

The compliment brought joy and I let my smile rip. "Aww baby, you're too sweet." I spanked his butt then held his shoulders and hopped up, wrapping my legs around his waist. He caught me and held my butt with his hands, making me blush.

"Perfect, love." His fingers pressed into my ass and he tossed a sexy look over his shoulder that made my stomach flip.

"I don't get it. How do we know who wins this? I mean what's the competition to know who wins the right to Dom in the... next phase?"

Ol' Girl gave that giggle, the one that spelled how dense I was. "If you manage to collect the ten flags at the top, you win the right to Dom next."

"Next as in..."

"As in the bedroom. For the night challenge." She bounced her perfectly sculpted brows.

Shit I needed to win that. I did not need to have Lucian Dom me. God help me sweet Jesus. I was losing my soul in this goddamn game. My soul and my mind. And my body. He was slowly taking it all and making me into something… something entirely different.

"Ready, love?"

"Ready."

****

"Be careful!" Tara cried.

I stopped climbing and sighed. "Love? Yell in my ear one more time and I'll drop you off of this mountain."

"Sorry, I'm trying to help."

"Then quit strangling me."

Two more steps and she blasted my ear with, "Are you tired? Just stop for a second and rest."

"We're being timed, love. Bad enough we're likely the only two who didn't get the questions right."

"Well it's not my fault! Her whole *body*? Who says that?"

"I do." A stray branch dug into my kneecap, nearly ending the race and our lives.

"I see that," Tara went on, oblivious. "And I lied about my answer, for your information."

Good grief. "No you didn't."

She choked on her annoyance. "Yes. I did. I don't care about a man's butt."

"Really."

"Really."

"So what is the real answer?" I paused, catching my breath and waiting.

"I'm not telling."

She dug her pointy heels into my upper thighs for emphasis. "Stop screeching in my ear like a fucking banshee." I started climbing again. "I think I know exactly what body part you like. You like a big thick cock."

"Oh yes, yes, I love that, sure I do."

"Say it. Cock."

"No!" More heel jabbing.

I laughed. "You're such a tender-minded princess. I can't wait to punish you for being bad today."

"What? Bad! Because I got the answer wrong?"

I laughed. "No, because you're disrespectful, and you're very, very bad at submitting. And it's time I help you with that."

Words choked up in her throat but she finally got them out. "Not if I win."

My cock throbbed with the anticipation. "Right." I continued to climb until searing pain seized my calf and nearly brought me down. "Jesus Christ!"

"What?" She squirmed in the carrying harness they'd strapped to my back.

"Cramp." I gritted my teeth and shifted, forcing my calf muscle to stretch slow and steady.

"Oh no! Where?" She moved again, leaning to my bad side nearly taking us down, while her arms tightened around my neck.

"Stop choking me!" I loosened her grip so I could breathe.

"Oh! Sorry. You're almost there, you only have like..."

"I can see, love. Fuck. Ugh." I concentrated on pulling the spasm out of my calf muscle. All Tara's wiggling about had shifted the carrying harness, causing a shoulder strap to cut into my collar bone.

"Guess your Wheaties are running out?"

"Yes, and your feathers are weighing a ton." I moved on as she gave a little snorting laugh that made me smile, and somehow lightened the load.

We finally made it to the top where the team of experts and Tara's favorite blonde waited. While they strapped us into climbing gear and anchored us to safety lines, I stared at the video monitor a technician was using to guide what looked like a radio-controlled helicopter with a camera attached. He moved the helicopter below the edge of the cliff, and the monitor filled with a view of crumbling rock. Slowly, a metal pole appeared in the frame, embedded in the stone. The camera moved out to reveal a small black flag fluttering madly from a hook at the end. For a split second, the flag stilled, just long enough for me to make out the words *DOM Wars* in white print.

The blonde took up a position well back from the edge of the cliff, a second tech standing opposite her with a small video camera. "Good afternoon, DOM Wars viewers! Today's challenge is in a slightly different format than you're accustomed to, in part because it's being streamed to you live. Thus far, both our contestants, and you, have been given very little information about the reasons behind the challenges. Today, that changes." She paused for the tech to make some adjustments. "Let's check in with Lucian and Tara as they prepare to face the newest phase in DOM Wars."

Her customary stilettos had been replaced by a pair of custom western boots, while painted-on jeans and a fitted leather vest took over for the usual business attire. With the cameraman following, she strode the few feet to where Tara and I were finishing up.

"Ready for the details?"

No, but we nodded anyway.

"Tara, you are going to *dangle* off the edge of that cliff, while you *trust* Lucian to hold you. Ten flags are already there, some more difficult to reach than others. You will retrieve as many as you can. If you get them all, you win the right to Dom. But don't worry, each flag you get is worth points, so each one counts for something even if you don't win the round. Any flags you drop before you're hauled back up here won't count. Questions?"

Tara nodded, and I really wanted to shake her, but it was too late to warn her not to ask anything. "What does this have to do with being a Dom?"

The announcer's brow lifted a little. "In the coming weeks, both you and our viewers will grow to deeper understanding. For now, suffice to say, any relationship, whether vanilla, D/s, platonic friendship, coworkers, or whatever, needs trust to be successful. The true Dom is an expert at both instilling trust in others, and in assessing whether others are worthy of trust. Our challenges are designed to show that process from both points of view."

To her credit, Tara listened carefully, obviously searching for some advantage, or even just rhyme or reason in the explanation.

"Okay, let's do this." The lady stepped back. "Good luck to you both."

The mountaineering experts that had prepared us came forward again and led us to the edge. Over the next five minutes, they gave us a crash course in exactly what we needed to do. Apparently deciding we were as ready as they could get us, they snapped our riggings into a series of bolts anchored deep in the rock under our feet, wished us luck and stepped back.

"Jesus, this is unfair. Why did you have to run your mouth this morning and mess me up?" Tara's words and tone were filled with dread and a dash of barely controlled panic.

I looked out over the ledge and fear pushed at my nerves. Twenty feet below, another narrow ledge strewn with jagged rocks reminded me of the crumbling, weathered stone I'd seen on the monitor. Below that, the cliff fell away for hundreds of feet, with death waiting and ready every inch of the way. My confidence in the material we were supposed to be anchored to for safety drained away. We were too fucking high. I looked at the ropes. They seemed sturdy but… this was Tara hanging over a fucking cliff. God, what if something happened and she fell? What if a carabiner broke? A freak accident?

Logically, I knew they'd doubled and tripled every conceivable safety precaution, but accidents were a fact of life. The breeze that had kept us comfortable earlier gave a sudden gust, whipping Tara's hair free of her pony-tail and across her face. Grumbling, she re-secured it.

Finally, the announcer gave us a two minute warning. I yanked hard on all the fittings at every point and double-checked that buckles were securely and completely fastened, and clips were closed, not caring that I looked like a mother hen. I wasn't taking any chances.

The countdown ended. Time to start. "Okay love, I'll be back here and you'll lean over—"

"I heard her! I know what to do, shush!" She shook her hands and breathed a few times. "Keep the line *very* tight! Please!"

"I got you baby. Line's staying tight." Fear flooded me and my muscles trembled with it. Shit. "Try to hurry and get it done."

"I can't *hurry!*" Exasperated, she inched next to the ledge. "Shit. It's so far, I'm going to have to lean Lucian!"

"I got you." No point in telling her that was the whole point. I concentrated on the rope in my hands.

"Hold me tight! I have to lean. Fuck, I have to lean. Oh God! Shit." The panic in her voice made me want to pull her back from that drop and carry her back down the mountain and keep her safe.

"Just lean baby and I'll slowly let you go forward, okay?"

"Oh God."

"Are you leaning?" Damn it, why wouldn't they just let her rappel to reach the flags? Why *lean* face first?

"I think. I think."

"I'm going to let some slack very slowly into the rope."

"Slowly!" she screamed. "Lucian, I'm scared."

Her fear fucking pummeled me. "I have you!" I yelled back firmly.

"Don't fuss at me, don't fuss at me," she whimpered.

"I'm not fussing at you baby, I'm sorry. You're doing fucking great. Can you reach it yet?"

She stretched. "Not yet. Oh God."

"How much further, one foot?"

"Yes, maybe. Maybe two?" She whimpered again, reaching for the damn flag.

"Okay, little bit more, love."

"Okay, okay, I can almost reach it!" Triumph filled her voice. "I got it! Pull me up!" Her cries of nervous victory echoed off the rocks surrounding us as I pulled her up

She ran and wrapped her arms around me tight. The flags were suddenly too incredibly stupid to repeat the insanity. "You can quit baby, you don't have to get anymore." I cradled her head to my chest grateful for her pulse fluttering against my palm where it pressed on her neck.

"I'm fine. I'm fine." She nodded and pushed away, going back to the edge. "We can do this. I'm ready. I'm ready, lean me."

I got back in place and repeated the process. She had to lean a little further, but it was okay. That first success had given her confidence to do whatever needed done. We did it again. And again. She was doing so well, beaming with each victory. But the rationalist in me only became more afraid. Every success put us that much closer to that one in a million chance of failing.

On the seventh flag, just as her fingers brushed against the plastic, my fucking foot slid on the loose gravel, throwing me off balance.

Tara jolted forward several inches. "Lucian!" Terror laced her scream and tore my guts.

"Fuck, baby!" I pulled her up, not caring about gentle, and hurried to wrap her in my arms. "I'm so sorry, my foot slipped."

Every part of her body trembled. "I can't. I can't do it. I'm so sorry, I just can't."

"Okay, okay." I glared at the blonde announcer and gave her a thumbs down, signaling we were done, then went back to comforting Tara. "You were fucking amazing, baby! You got *seven* flags."

"I got seven?" A broad grin spread across her face, even while tears of horror spilled over her lower lashes. "I did, I got seven!"

I held her closer, stroking her head. "I'm so proud of you, you're my angel." I turned her face up and planted my lips firmly on hers, desperate to kiss away her fears.

Chapter Three

Back in our mini-dungeon, I watched Lucian from the kitchen table. Silent Lucian. Far too quiet since we were brought back from the challenge. *Take your shower while I cook.* Oh, I'd showered well. In my head, I prayed he would go easy on me, while my body trembled with other prayers I didn't want to even contemplate.

The food smelled amazing, onions and beef making my mouth water. Too bad my stomach was in so many knots, eating would be impossible. Lucian wearing nothing but black BVDs didn't help at all. The sight of him was hard to ignore.

He was Dom tonight, but he was mixing the signals, confusing me. Cooking. Being gentle. Sweet. What did it all mean? Maybe he felt bad about screwing up the last challenge with that foot slip. Maybe he planned to let me off the hook. I could use a break.

My stomach tensed as he came to the table with a plate of food. And sat with it. Across from me. I waited to see what he had in mind. He began cutting the steak. Had I been way off base? Was he pissed at me for something and now would punish me with no food? Anger began to slowly burn up my spine at just the thought.

He reached across the small table with the forkful of steak. He was feeding me? Confusion chased away my anger as I looked at the food, suddenly sure I couldn't eat. "I'm... not that hungry."

"You haven't eaten since breakfast, love."

The tenderness in his voice held something else. An edge of... something. "Near death experiences have a way of stealing my appetite."

He stared at me for several seconds.

What was going through that mind of his? Nerves forced me to speak, to apologize. "Sorry. Maybe... I'll feel hungry later?"

He put the bite slowly in his mouth, keeping his pretty blue eyes focused directly on me. The beginnings of a beard shadowed his face and the rugged look seemed to grind against my female parts. He chewed slowly, staring at me and I was suddenly caught. Caught in his silent trap of mind-blowing sex appeal.

I had to watch him chew, had to watch his mouth. God his lips. Part of me realized he knew exactly what he was doing, deliberately calculating his effect on me and using it, and yet I couldn't stop it from being done to me. Could he seduce my body and mind with something as simple as eating? Yes. Yes he certainly could. And was.

The tip of his tongue swept over his lower lip, making my stomach flip. The slight shine there brought my appetite slamming in, but not for food.

Dear God, help me, I was in trouble. Everything about the way he looked, the way he moved and didn't move, spelled trouble in all caps. Literally. Because I'd finally made out that unfamiliar thing in his mood. It was definitely the calm before the storm. Like aftercare before he ever began. The air around him was filled with *you've been so bad, love. And I'm going to tear through you like a tragic storm on a still morning.*

He slid the plate away, another deliberate act. Calm. Calculated. "You know what's coming."

My clit literally throbbed with those all-knowing hot words.

"You can start with thanking me."

I stared at him, speechless, trying to feel something besides the crippling need to be touched by him. Thank him? I needed to thank him? My mind said I could be angry with that, should be even. I stared like a dumb lamb, fumbling with the matches to light that little stick of angry dynamite. But everything was too wet. Drenched.

He stood and my eyes held tight to him. He held his hand out and I took it without even thinking. And then he led and I followed. All so strange, it was like a dream.

"I'm going to be nice and let you choose. From that shelf."

I looked at the shelf he pointed to, the one holding a selection of dildos. A bolt of heat speared me. Followed hard with the realization that the ones on that shelf were all double, each with a smaller one attached. Dear God. Fear finally kicked in and raced to catch up. I shook my head a little.

"Tara."

I closed my eyes at the warning in his voice. So many warnings. The one carrying the most weight in my mind wasn't how badly we needed the points to win. It was how badly he needed to do this. Had to. But I couldn't choose. I couldn't. "Please." Pick for me, I can't. That's what needed saying.

His face was suddenly before me as I looked at him, gentle hands on either side of my head, tender lips on mine. "Fuck, love. Don't look at me that way. Your fear is killing me." Hot breath melted me, so full of agony and need. "I want so badly to crush it. Let me. Let me inside of you."

My answer came in helpless whimpers and I could only hope he understood it. *Do what you need,* I wanted to say, scream, anything. But it was his need I was answering. God, it was so pure and perfect and, Jesus, hot. But my body refused to hook up to my mind. It was trapped in two different worlds, standing there helpless at a surreal crossroads set on fire by Lucian Bane.

The flames licked hot along my mind and body. *Surrender. Surrender.* I wanted to give in to his… whatever it was, whatever he was. He was a thousand suns in my eyes, I couldn't see anything but his blinding light, couldn't feel anything except his scorching heat.

I was dying a strange death. And terrified. It was that death I didn't want, but needed. I could feel it. I longed for it, craved it, loathed it, abhorred it, ran from it, Jesus Christ.

He lifted me in his arms and I clung to him. Buried my face in his neck. Clenched my eyes against the raging need, the fear. I continued to hide when he laid me down. He restrained me with silk ties. My arms first. Softly. Slowly. Then my ankles.

I didn't fight him. Not once. I didn't resist. Not even when he stretched my legs so very wide. Not even when soft silk covered my eyes.

"I'm going to adore you, love." His whisper stirred my hair and tickled my ear to send a combination of chills and sparks darting over my skin. "Every bit of you. With all my being. With all my might."

He began that contract at my lips. Tasting them with nibbling reverence until I opened in desperate hunger, my breath fighting to keep up with the emotion he provoked. His fingers glided along my out-stretched arms, his naked body skimming mine. The whisper of reckless passion, coming hard and fast on the horizon.

His lips slid to my chin, then slowly along my jaw. He moved his body so that the hot length of his cock stroked along my inner thigh. At my neck, he licked with a deep moan of hunger. I answered him with my own.

"I know, God, I know." His lips slid across my chest. "You need this, love. For so long."

I cried out at the hot suction on my breast followed by his warm breath and scrape of his teeth. "Lucian." His name burst forth, like freedom. I pulled on my restraints and arched my back, seeking his mouth. "Please."

He answered with a groan of agony, his mouth wet and hot on my other breast, his tongue licking and flicking, his lips gliding, teeth scraping. His fingers were everywhere, brushing softly then scratching, his cock pressing at the juncture of wide open thighs. I lifted my hips for it.

He was suddenly back at my mouth, his cock sliding between my folds. "That what you want baby?" He slid himself along my clit.

"God, yes."

His breath shuddered in my mouth and his fingers danced over my clit. "I need to suck this into my mouth first. Lick it until you're nearly undone." He slid his fingers lower to my entrance and plunged his finger deep inside me. "I need to fill you up, fill you up completely." I bucked against his hand and he glided his finger to my butt. "Baby." He pressed his finger on the opening. "I have to lick this. Then fuck it with my tongue." He pushed the tip into me. "You want that, love?" He nibbled at my lower lip then sucked it between his. "I'm so fucking crazy for you. You need to know that."

He was suddenly feasting on my breasts again, the sound of a man on the edge, groaning, winded, his fingers biting and urgent. He gripped my waist and fear seized me. "I-I need to see you."

His fingers slowly went slack and he whispered his hands up my body, following with his lips until he was back at my mouth. He slid the blindfold off while kissing me, his fingers stroking along my face, along my hair. "I'm here, love. It's all me, always."

****

She wanted to see me. Fuck, the things that did to me. And I'd nearly said forever. All me, always me. Forever. I'd used the blindfold thinking it would be easier for her. But she needed to see me. She needed me. Dear God, fuck yes.

I couldn't devour her fast enough now. I so needed her to see me. See me break her down. See how much I fucking loved it. How did she always do this? Every time I made plans, she'd say one thing, make one sound and wreck it in the most profound way. The most beautiful way. Back between her thighs, I gripped her ass and lifted her. One thing had not changed. My insatiable need to make her scream with pleasure.

I stroked my lips softly along her open folds, digging fingers into her ass muscles, while fighting to hold on to my sanity. Up and down her length I slid my mouth until her scent made me ravenous, her fucking incessant cries had me insane. "Jesus Christ, fuck!" I plunged my tongue into her dripping entrance and pressed my nose all over that sweet hard clit. I was lost, fuck. I moved to her cute ass and licked all over it.

"Yes, yes! Lucian!"

"God-fucking-damn," I gasped, working my tongue into her ass. I pulled and pushed her on me until she trembled everywhere with need. She needed to be filled up. But God I didn't want a fucking dildo doing it. I wanted to see her come everywhere while my cock filled her and my finger fucked her ass.

I stopped and retied her hands together on the head board. Knees apart, ass up, face down, Jesus Christ, yes.

I stroked my hands over her hips. "Baby, I'm going to fuck you now. Are you ready for it, love?"

She nodded rapidly. "Yes, yes."

I held her perfect fucking hips and slid very slowly inside her. "You feel me baby? Filling you up?"

She cried out, nodding.

I groaned hard when I reached bottom. "I'm all the way in baby." The words blasted with my desire. I fought to catch my breath as I watched. "I look so fucking good buried in you." I tickled the tip of my pinky at her tight ass and she gave a sharp cry, drawing my finger in. "Yes baby. You like that, fuck."

"Yes, yes. Fuck me Lucian. God please, just do it."

"Oh God," I groaned, closing my eyes against the raging orgasm her words provoked. She flicked her hips and I worked my finger deeper inside her.

"Oh my God, Lucian."

"I'm gonna, baby, fuck wait." I got my finger halfway in and pulled my cock slowly out. "God, love..." I let out a long hiss. "You're all over my cock. So wet. So beautiful." I stroked along her spine with my other hand while sliding my length slowly back inside. "Are you ready to get fucked love?"

"Jesus, yes."

She was frantic. Just like I had to have her. "Do it. Move your pussy on me." I worked my finger in and out, and reached beneath her with my other hand. "Your clit baby. So hard. So hot isn't it?"

"God, yes Lucian."

"I know baby. That's it, fuck my cock." I rolled my hips when she worked herself all the way on me, growling on the urge to tear into her. "You're so close, I can feel it."

"I'm coming Lucian. I'm coming! Lucian, Jesus--"

I thrust in deep and began bucking my hips. "Fucking come all over me." I rammed my cock in and out, jerking her, wiggling my finger over her clit, moving my finger in her ass.

She began to sing out this fucking orgasm that grew in intensity as her body shook and trembled and bucked. So beautiful. I growled through the onslaught of pleasure, determined not to orgasm, not yet. Not fucking yet, not like this. I needed her beneath me, our bodies pressed together hard, I needed her voice in my ear, in my mouth, my cock buried as deep as it could go. That's what I needed.

I slowed my strokes, sliding my hand up and down her spine, caressing her ass with the other, listening to her soft lingering cries of astonishment. I pulled out and untied her. She rolled onto her side, still winded, and stared at my cock. Seeing I wasn't done, she flushed with desire again. I stood next to the bed, watching it slither through her limbs until it opened her legs, undulated her hips, arched her spine, and hardened her perfect nipples. Good fucking God.

I crawled on the bed until my body was prone to hers. She held my gaze and fuck, tears filled her eyes.

"What, love?" My heart raced hard in my chest.

"I'm sorry."

"For what?" I leaned and kissed her lips softly, not wanting anything to ruin what I'd just given her.

"For..." she looked off to the left, her chin trembling, "...losing the game."

"Fuck, love, I slipped, it wasn't your fault. It was mine."

"I know, and I freaked."

"*You* freaked? Love, if you had been in my head, I nearly had a heart attack."

She raised her brows then snickered. "You did?"

"Fuck, yes! I was so glad you quit. I'm not kidding."

She stared at me until her face became a severe mask of nothing I could identify or justify her having in that second. What had I said? She grabbed my face and pulled me to her mouth and wrapped her legs around my waist. "Make love to me. Please."

Her words with the desperate way she moved to them knocked me on my ass. I fumbled like a teenager to comply and the second I found her entrance, she jerked my hips and buried me deep inside her.

The cry she gave pierced my fucking heart, Jesus Christ. I kissed her, if you could call devouring another person that. But I'd never been so hungry to have every part of somebody the way I wanted her. And the way she seemed to return the feeling, holy fuck, it undid me. The next thing I knew she flipped us, putting her on top. I held her waist and watched her, forced her tight to my groin and rolled my hips, hitting her core with the head of my cock. Fuck, yes, she liked that. Seeing her on me like that, brought my orgasm like a runaway comet, there was no fucking denying it. I kept her tight to me, grinding the head of my cock deep with hard jerks until my body locked up with ecstasy, blinding fucking ecstasy. I bowed up off the bed and she sealed her chest to mine, her cries in my mouth as I wrapped my arms around her.

Fuck, she'd just done something to me. I didn't know what it was, I only knew I was never going to be the same again.

A QUICK WORD OR TWO

ABOUT BDSM

A quick word about real life BDSM and the lifestyle, particularly,
CONTRACTS

Why am I picking contracts? Because if you're considering them,
then it can't hurt to get as much information as you can since
contracts are taken very seriously by many who negotiate and sign
them in the "Lifestyle."

And please keep in mind as you read, that everything I say here will
not apply to you and your situation. It is only my intent to cover as
many angles as I can in case there is that one person reading who
may be vulnerably new to the lifestyle, or even trapped in a possibly
unsafe situation, needing and seeking guidance or answers.

First of all…. let me start with saying this: The "Lifestyle" can apply
to any couple, whether they are hardcore 24/7 practitioners of
BDSM in varying types and degrees, or just a random couple who
dabble only on occasion. And regardless of which category you fall
under, the contract protocol—whether written or merely spoken—
should **ALWAYS** be applied.

Let's talk about the "Lifestyle" and its three main governing rules.

Whether you're hardcore or just curious after reading a BDSM
related book by one of your favorite authors, the main three
governing rules are easy to find in a Google search.

And they are:

SAFE

SANE
CONSENSUAL

Now honestly, you shouldn't even be considering negotiating a contract with anybody without first sitting down with them and establishing what those 3 words above, mean to both of you. You can't SAFELY or SANELY negotiate anything when words like "safe" "sane" and "consensual" are subjective terms and could mean different things to different people. For instance, they may find it completely sane to leave you tied up or do other things you don't want or like because after all, you consented. And maybe to them, you can't change your mind because that would mean you're breaking your contract or your word.
(I'll talk more about when and how to re-negotiate contracts below)

Or maybe you didn't agree to a particular thing but because "safe" to them means only physical safety, they might exempt your emotional and mental well-being from that NECESSARY

"Lifestyle Protocol". After all, they may consider it just a "game" or "play".
I'm very sure if your daughter, friend, or any loved one were contemplating signing a contract of this nature, you could think of many other ways that the words "safe" "sane" and "consensual" could be misconstrued, whether intentional or just ignorantly, thereby NECESSITATING establishing and agreeing on what those words should mean to the parties involved. In fact, when reading over a proposed contract, I would **STRONGLY** advise you to pretend that the contract is for your daughter or best friend. This will enable you to "see beyond" your own emotions and feelings for the person you're entering a contract with. Every line of the contract, say to yourself, "What would I say to this if it were my daughter/best friend?"

So, once you're both on the same page as best as you can be about the meaning of those three **GOVERNING** Lifestyle laws, consider what negotiating a contract actually mean?
Some who enter the Lifestyle don't even KNOW that they should be involved in the negotiation of a contract and instead allow only one party to propose negotiation to which they feel they must agree and sign.

THAT IS AN OUTRIGHT BREECH OF LIFESTYLE PROTOCOL! IF YOU ARE ASKED TO DO THAT, LEAVE IMMEDIATELY.

Common sense should NEVER escape you in any aspect of your life, not even if all of this BDSM stuff is for "oh funsies" to you. Because more times than not, the "oh funsies" approach can turn into an "oh fucksies," all because you neglected to use your God-given common sense. And signing a contract without negotiating it would certainly fall under mega-stupid and could very likely lead you straight into that "oh fuck, what have I done" moment you **NEVER** want to find yourself in.

LET KNOWLEDGE BE YOUR WEAPON

LET PREVENTION BE YOUR SHIELD

SEXUAL ABUSE HAPPENS EVERYWHERE BUT THE LIFESTYLE IS RAMPANT WITH

PREDATORS WHO WILL EXPLOIT YOUR GOODNESS UNTIL YOU CAN'T

REMEMBER WHAT IT IS TO BE A HUMAN BEING!

ONLY YOU CAN PREVENT THIS FROM HAPPENING!

So, to conclude this section of contracts, it is NECESSARY that BOTH PARTIES contribute to the devising of a contract.

So let's continue with what SAFE~SANE~ and CONSENSUAL mean.

Beginning with SAFE...
Being SAFE mostly means remembering to use your common sense. I would have to write an entire book on how many things to not allow in a contract and for time's sake, I'm going to point you once again to a rule of thumb that will reduce a lot of bullshit and that is—read it as though it is being proposed to your daughter or best friend. You will be surprised to see how objectionable and smart you can be in that mindset. After that, you give the contract to several people to read and have them tear it apart to see if you are missing anything that could be detrimental.

(And honestly, I don't endorse entering a contract with a Dom that doesn't intend to be committed to you. In that respect, I may be considered a freak by many in the lifestyle, but in my experience, the truest and most powerful kind of Dom, is the man that is not afraid to love ONE woman with all his heart, mind, and strength. A Dom that is willing to give HIMSELF in the same measure he expects of his own sub. If you are entering a contract with a person who does not hold to these kinds of convictions, you run the risk of getting hurt, and you need to know that up front. Does this make men who marry their subs better than other men? No. They can still be manipulative just the same, maybe even more so. But to enter a contract with a man who openly says "I'm not going to give you my heart" seems a tad fucking foolish to me. If he's not going to give you his heart, then what the fuck are you getting? A human dildo? You're worth much, **MUCH,** more than that, and if you don't agree with me then you DEFINITELY don't need to be looking into getting into a BDSM contract. Because Subs with low, or no self-esteem are the most common victims of ABUSE.

You can prevent that by:
KNOWING YOUR WORTH

and

GETTING THE SAME COMMITMENT AND DEVOTION FROM YOUR DOM/PARTNER THAT THEY EXPECT TO GET FROM YOU.

NEXT:

WHAT DOES SANE MEAN?

Sane means that whatever you put in that contract will not cause an individual to endure anything contrary to basic, current, psychological and physiological health.

Keep in mind that BDSM is a tool that can bring a couple closer together and build intimate bonds. BUT it also can and is, a very easy means to abuse. MANY people use BDSM to gradually condition their partners to move deeper and deeper into sadism and masochism. Sometimes this happens without meaning to, sometimes it's intentional. The danger with indulging in sadism and masochistic activities is the pleasure addiction threshold dynamic. You start out safe and sane and then the pleasure threshold will move a little farther away, requiring more to stimulate pleasure. This is where it can get dangerous. But if you both have a knowledgeable handle on how those sexual mechanisms work and can evolve and grow, you can put boundaries to prevent problems (assuming both parties are sane people)

So, when devising the boundaries in a contract, remember that. Talk about it openly. Even if either parties are not prone to sadistic or masochistic pleasures, those can and often do grow with engagement. Some forms of play can awaken drives that were not there or dormant. The SANE key here is knowing this is a risk and to always keep your eyes open for signs of things moving in a bad direction.

NEXT:

WHAT DOES CONSENSUAL MEAN?

This is really one to be exploited. Many will say "well he/she wanted it" And suddenly the "CONSENSUAL" takes precedence over SAFE and SANE. If that happens, they have violated SAFE and SANE protocol and need to get out or stop the program/game/whatever you call it, immediately.

CONTRACTS ALWAYS SHOULD BE…EVEN AFTER SIGNING THEM—NEGOTIABLE!

There are NO hard fast rules about ANY contract. A contract in this sense, is a UNIQUE agreement between UNIQUE people and not ONE of them should look the same. They should reflect the needs/desires/wants of those two unique individuals under the SAFE/SANE/CONSENSUAL umbrella.

What does this mean? This means that if at any time you realize that you want something different in the contract, you should be able to say "hey, I'm not liking such and such and would like to talk about changing that to something less this or more that" and at that point, the other party should say "Of course." And that's IT.

The other thing I want you to understand about contracts is their practicality. It's more like a **GUIDE** or a **RULE** book that would explain and agree how the parties involved want to "live" the lifestyle in all sincerity, or just "play" it on occasion. And the binding aspect of the contract demonstrates the level of **COMMITMENT** one plans to give to those things agreed on in the contract.

So basically, you've got things in the contract like: what you're willing to do, what you're willing to try or not try, how you're going to do or try, how much, how long, whatever you feel is important to include must be put in the contract. You establish boundaries and "safe cues" (a word you say or something you do so the other party knows you want to quit or stop and discuss how to change things). If you're thinking at this point… *What if I don't know what to include or not include? What if I can't foresee the bad things?* Then you're being smart, because that is a very valid point to be thinking.

Contracts of this nature SHOULD ALWAYS CONTAIN SOME KIND OF CLAUSE FOR RE-NEGOTIATION.

Those in committed relationships usually have what I would call a floating contract, meaning its details should be allowed to change as the couple's explore and learn one another. Both parties are PRONE to this type of change because they are in a relationship, and relationships are **living**, **breathing** and **evolving** things. It would be difficult to the point of ridiculous to have certain details set in stone when the playing fields involved are the hearts, minds, and bodies of two unique people that are designed to CHANGE as they GROW and become ONE.

If you're thinking this sounds a lot like a marriage, then you'd be right. That's exactly how marriages work or should work.

I'd like to point out an interesting fact many may not be aware of here. And that is how the biblical definition of marriage matches the D/s lifestyle nearly to a T. Basically, the "lifestyle" as many know it today, has existed **long** before they ever thought to call it a "lifestyle". So, don't let **ANYBODY** try to tell you what you have to do and what you can't do in order to be in the "lifestyle" They don't **OWN** the rules or the lifestyle. The lifestyle is a template **FOR** the people to adapt to their needs. People are **not** to change to fit **other** people's notions and ideas about the lifestyle, rather the lifestyle is designed to change and fit "people", under the safe, sane, and consensual protocols.

So, the contract should involve the basics, and leave the things that are prone to change (individual wants, needs, desires) open to growth without having to constantly renegotiate.
SO:

DO NOT EVER SIGN OVER ALL CONTROL IN THE NEGOTIATION ASPECT!

Some Dom/Dommes want absolute control over their subs and ask for them to turn over ALL CONTROL. It is one thing to sign over control in some aspects but **NEVER** over the aspect of re-negotiation. That would NOT be considered a contract, that would be a **DEATH NOTE**.

LAST BUT NOT LEAST

MANIPULATION

Sometimes manipulation is employed on partners in a passive and maybe even subconscious way, and other times it's outright bullying. Any form of manipulation upon another person's will in order to get that which the person does not wish to give, is WRONG. DON'T PUT UP WITH IT.
If you are already in a contract, whether written or just agreed verbally to, and you feel like you HAVE to do things that you're not comfortable with, then you are being manipulated and abused. You should seek outside help from a trusted advisor.

(There are exceptions to this "comfort zone" as with a person recovering from past abuse, both sexual and non. In some cases, the couple may gently help one another to overcome bondage that past abuse put upon them. And those cases, pushing the comfort zone is done to help free their mind, heart, and body from the prison the abuse holds them in. For this reason, it's imperative they gently push the comfort zones so that they can re-learn and reclaim what is considered "healthy sexual activity". And for your information, sadism, masochism, sado-masochism, and other similar sexual fetishes in certain degrees, are deemed not healthy by the medical profession, and nobody should be "pushed" into engaging in those things beyond what is safe and sane.

Last Thing:

LOVE

That's a word you don't see thrown around much in the current "lifestyle" sad to say.

Why is that a problem?

Loving your partner, whether with a basic, human love, or wife/husband love, is an ESSENTIAL ingredient that is REQUIRED to maintain the all-important, SAFE and SANE rules. If love does not exist between the couple—then your risk of being subjected to insane and unsafe scenarios is nearly guaranteed.

When there is an absence of base, human components like compassion, understanding, patience, and empathy—harm is sure to follow. Humans are designed to thrive under those conditions and are guaranteed to slowly (maybe even quickly, depending on the degree) die under anything else.

I'd like to wrap this up with the following:

To the person or persons reading this who are considering entering a relationship involving a contract…

Remember who you are.
You are a *woman*.
And you are *so* beautiful, do you hear me?

You *must* hear me.
You are worth more than riches could ever buy in a million years.
Without you, this world would not exist or continue to exist.
We *need* you.
You are *so needed.*
And if you don't *feel* this profound truth within yourself, then something is wrong.
Because you should.
If you don't look in the mirror and like who you see, what you see, then something is wrong.
And *you* are the only one that holds the power to make it right.

YOU. ARE THE HERO. TO. THE. WORLD.

So be the hero in **YOUR** world.
You're *beautiful*.
You're *smart.*
And **YOU. CAN. DO IT.**

Love Lucian

Made in the USA
Monee, IL
01 February 2024

52763962R00128